Astragal

ASTRAGAL

Albertine Sarrazin

Translated from the French by Patsy Southgate

Introduction by Patti Smith

A NEW DIRECTIONS BOOK

First published by New Directions as NDP1250 in 2013
Published simultaneously in Canada by Penguin Books Canada Limited
Manufactured in the United States of America
New Directions Books are printed on acid-free paper.
Design by Erik Rieselbach

10 9 8 7 6 5 4 3 2 1

New Directions Books are published for James Laughlin
by New Directions Publishing Corporation
80 Eighth Avenue. New York 10011

Contents

My Albertine

Perhaps it is wrong to speak of oneself while writing of another, but I truly wonder if I would have become as I am without her. Would I have carried myself with the same swagger, or faced adversity with such feminine resolve, without Albertine as my guide? Would my young poems have possessed such a biting tongue without *Astragal* as my guidebook?

I discovered her, quite unexpectedly, while roaming Greenwich Village in 1968. It was All Saints Day, a fact that I later noted in my journal. I was hungry and craved coffee, but first ducked into the Eighth Street Bookshop to inspect the reduced fare on the remainder tables. They held stacks of *Evergreen Review*s and obscure translations from Olympia and Grove Press—new scriptures shunned by the populace. I was on the lookout for something I had to have: a book that was more than a book, containing certain signs that might spin me toward an unforeseen path. I was drawn to a striking, remote face—rendered violet on black—on a dust jacket proclaiming its author "a female Genet." It cost ninety-nine cents, the price of a grilled cheese and coffee at the Waverly Diner, just across Sixth Avenue. I had a dollar and a subway token, but after reading the first few lines I was smitten—one hunger trumped another and I bought the book.

The book was *Astragal*, and the face on the cover belonged to Albertine Sarrazin. Returning to Brooklyn by train, devouring the meager flap copy, I learned only that she was born in Algiers, was orphaned, had served time and had written two books in prison and one in freedom, and had recently died, in 1967, just shy of her thirtieth birthday. Finding and losing a potential sister all in the same moment touched me deeply. I was approaching twenty-two, on my own, estranged from Robert Mapplethorpe. It was to be a harsh winter, having left the warmth of certain arms for the uncertainty of others. My new love was a painter, who would come unannounced, read passages aloud from *Our Lady of the Flowers*, make love to me, and then disappear for weeks on end.

These were the nights of one hundred sleeps: nothing could appease my restless agitation. Trapped in the distracting drama of waiting—for the muse, for him—was a malicious torment. My own words were not enough, only another's could transform misery into inspiration.

In *Astragal* I found the words, written by a girl eight years older than me, now dead. There was no entry for her in the encyclopedia, so I had to piece her together (as I had Genet) through her every syllable, with the understanding that a poet's memoirs must move through falsehoods in order to unmask the truth. I fired up some coffee, propped the pillows on my bed, and began to read. *Astragal* was the bone that fused fact and fiction.

Sentenced to seven years for armed robbery, Anne, a girl of nineteen, jumps over the prison wall—a thirty-foot drop. She cracks her ankle in the process and beneath a myriad of pitiless stars is seemingly helpless. Tiny but tough, she drags herself across the pavement, inching her way toward the road. She is mercifully scooped up by another soul on the lam, a petty thief named Julien. She clocks him and knows he's done time; he exudes that ex-con scent. They make their way through the bone-chilling night on his motorcycle. Before dawn he lays her child body tenderly in the childbed of a contact. Later she is moved to the upstairs room of a disgruntled and suspicious family, then again to a friend of a friend. That's how it goes—her so-called liberation—getting deposited in a series of hideouts.

She writes of bouts of restiveness. What kind of sleeps did she have? Were they sounder in prison, not having to look over her shoulder? How was it to sleep on the lam, wondering if narrowed eyes revealed soon-to-be open betrayal? Her bum leg is encased in plaster, but even more painful is the startling fact that Julien has cracked open her hustler heart. Her intense longing for him is a kind of jail term of its own. She has no choice but to endure being shifted around. Hermes with an ankle, bent and broken, cruelly tattooed with a mercurial wing drained of speed.

The heroine is condemned to wait for her precious hoodlum. Trials, missteps, incarcerations, and small joys constitute their story. They are characters from the life of a book that she has written. I pictured her no longer lame but free, in a straight skirt and sleeveless blouse tied above her waistline, with a wisp of chiffon around her throat. She was under five feet tall, but she was no trembling waif—more like a stick of dynamite that in exploding might not kill, but would certainly maim. Her ability to size up a situation, to read a john or her lover's every gesture is profound, her one-liners swift and cutting. "You wanted to burden me with your love." She possesses a lively slang of her own—an argot spattered with Latin.

A female Genet? She is herself. She possesses a unique highbrow poet-detective deadpan style: "I escaped near Easter but nothing was rising from the dead." This poetic perspicacity—"crafty and purified"—runs through her narrative like a narrow river breaking over the rocks; a dark vein crashing and rejoining. Albertine, the petite saint of maverick writers. How swiftly I was swept into her world—ready to scribble through the night, down pots of scalding coffee, and pause just long enough to reline the eyes with Maybelline. Her youthful mantra was wholeheartedly embraced, my malleable spirit infused.

"I want to leave, but where? Seduce, but who? Write, but what?"

In joining the legion of Albertine, it is necessary to salute the translator Patsy Southgate. In 1968 she was also under the radar—a stunning blonde with the ice-blue eyes of a husky who wrote and translated for the *Paris Review*. Finding a picture of her sitting in a Paris café having chopped her blonde tresses was a revelation. I taped it to my wall alongside Albertine, Falconetti, Edie Sedgwick, and Jean Seberg—girls with close-cropped hair, the girls of my day.

Patsy Southgate was an enigma. As a child of privilege and neglect, she instinctively knew just how to slip into *Astragal*, and may have felt a hidden kinship with her subject. She was intelligent, complicated, and passionately drawn to every rung of French culture: an expat darling of the post-beats and famously adored by Frank O'Hara. A lonely and severely disciplined child, she had a French governess named Louise who lavished more tenderness on her than her own parents. When

Louise returned to Paris to marry, Patsy was devastated: she spent much of her life longing for her imagined mother, the true mother of her invented French soul.

Within her fleeting life, Albertine also longed to know the identifty of her mother. Born and abandoned in 1937 in Algeria, she was given the name Albertine Damien by Social Services and baptized Anne-Marie when she was adopted. Her origins were always in question, and perhaps only a cluster of DNA samples could have revealed them. Was she the daughter of a teenage Spanish dancer and a sailor? Or was she the illegitimate child of her adoptive father and his Jewish-Algerian maid? Romance and controversy in either case, and a setup for a marginalized existence. She was a precocious little thing and by the merit of her gifts—she excelled in Latin, literature, and the violin—should have experienced a rich musical life and a scholarly education. But a lack of loving protection and a series of wrenching external events twisted her path forever.

At ten, she was raped by a member of her stepfather's family. After her attempts to run away, her parents placed her in a girl's reformatory paradoxically called The Good Shepherd. It was a wretched place where she was humiliated and stripped of her baptismal name of Anne-Marie. At thirteen she kept a spiral notebook, a precious record of her perceptive observances: it was confiscated when the lily-of-the-valley perfume she wore was deemed too strong. She was petite and pretty, armed with the discerning wit of Joan of Arc on trial, and she escaped from reform school and slipped into the Paris streets to eventually lead the life of a prostitute and petty thief. At eighteen she was arrested, with a female accomplice, for armed robbery and given seven years. Her last stint was four months in 1963 for pilfering a bottle of whiskey. Through it all she wrote: throughout her adolescence, through love and abandonment, in or out of prison, she wrote.

Life is often the best movie. Hers ended sadly, in a hospital, where she wearily smiled at Julien, then surrendered her fate to a negligent anesthesiologist. What dreams lay behind those heavy eyelids crowned with a Maybelline crescent, as she was wheeled away—a future with Julien, peace and prosperity, recognition? All was possible, for at last they were on the cusp. They had married, kissing crime good-bye. She exited the world loved, but also as she had entered it—on a cloud of neglect.

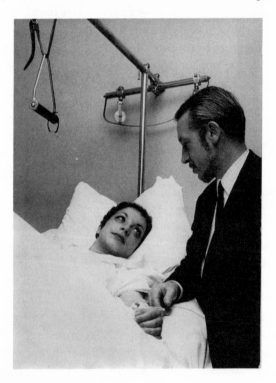

Saint Albertine of the disposable pen and the interminable eyebrow pencil. I lived in her atmosphere. I imagined the blue smoke of her cigarette curling around her nostrils, moving through her bloodstream and riding the chambers of her heart. I was too bronchial to smoke myself, but I carried a pack of *Gauloises vertes* in my skirt pocket. I paced the floors waiting for my painter to come and rescue me from my self-imposed prison, as she had waited for Julien. Never was the wait so bearable, nor Nescafé such an elixir. I created my own jargon, primed by *Astragal* and extended with *La Cavale*, her next novel, translated as *The Runaway*, with one of the great opening lines in French literature: "I am really done up for my entrance into prison tonight: opossum and slacks."

Abandoned by one hope, I found another in Sam Shepard. When we too had to part, we wrote our swan song in the form of the play *Cowboy Mouth*, and in homage to Albertine I named my character Cavale, a name that means escape, as she explains at the play's end.

In 1976, as I traveled the world, I carried *Astragal* in a small metal suitcase, filled with sweat-stained tee shirts, talismans, and the same black jacket I wore with careless defiance on the cover of *Horses*. It was a Black Cat paperback edition with a picture of Marlène Jobert on the cover. It cost 95 cents, roughly what I'd paid for the hardcover in 1968. I carried it to Detroit where I met my own true Julien—a complex, guarded, beautiful man who made me his bride and later his widow. After he died I brought *Astragal* back to New York with me in 1996, packed amongst a trove of bittersweet memories.

Before a recent tour of France, I unwittingly unearthed this same copy, but I could not bear to open it. Instead I wrapped it in an old handkerchief and carried it along in yet another metal suitcase. It was as if I had Albertine, a battered blossom, beneath my twenty-first century version of sweat-stained tee shirts. Then one waking night in a hotel in Toulouse I suddenly unwrapped it and once more began reading it, reliving the leap and the crack of lightning that was her ankle splitting and the headlights flashing as her angel examined her startled heart-shaped face. Scenes of my life commingled with her words with a muted force. And there, pressed between the yellowed pages, was an old picture of my love, and within its well-worn folds a lock of his lank brown hair—a precious relic of him within a relic of her.

Not passing angels but the angels of my life.

One day I shall visit her grave with a thermos of black coffee and sit with her a while and sprinkle lily-of-the-valley perfume on her headstone—in the shape of an astragal bone, which Julien had placed in remembrance. My Albertine, how I adored her! Her luminous eyes led me through the darkness of my youth. She was my guide through the nights of one hundred sleeps. And now she is yours.

PATTI SMITH

Astragal

1

The sky had lifted at least thirty feet.

I sat there, not moving. The shock must have cracked the pavement, my right hand fumbled in the rubble. As I breathed, the silence stilled the explosion of stars whose sparks still crackled in my head. The white lines in the pavement showed dimly in the darkness: my hand left the ground, felt up my left arm, up to my shoulder, back down my ribs to my hips: nothing, I was intact, I could go on.

I stood up. Falling flat on my face, sprawled out like a cross, I remembered that I had forgotten to check over my legs as well. Piercing the night, wise and familiar voices sang out at me:

"Careful, Anne, you'll wind up with a broken leg!"

I sat back up and began exploring myself again. This time, near my ankle, I ran into a strange swelling which puffed and throbbed beneath my fingers....

When I go to the infirmary, Doc, and try to fake an illness, and describe imaginary pains in places I think are inaccessible; when I have to bring tea up to you in bed, little sisters, I tiptoeing carefully, envying your stomachaches.... That's all over:

now you'll have to take care of me, you or someone else, I've busted my leg.

I raised my eyes to the top of the wall where that world still was, asleep: I've flown away, my dears! I flew and soared and wheeled around for one second which was long and good, a century. And here I am, sitting down here, safe from up there, safe from you.

Again this afternoon I was full of atropine and had injected some benzine into my thighs. Rolande was out, I had no intention of waiting around for her to come back and get me: I fixed it to have myself sent to the hospital, where the life would be softer and the days turned to dust more quickly.

"But you look green!" the matron says to me during the evening.

"I must have brushed up against the wall," I say, feeling my cheeks turn white, and twisting around as if trying to see the back of my blouse. We were just in the process of repainting the dining room, one wall yellow, one wall blue, two walls green, and the window ledges orange to look like the sun.

"No, it's you that's green, YOU! Your face! Do you feel all right?"

But I didn't wait to enjoy my first cup of tea; the gentle slope on the other side of the wall, beyond the gate, I would not go down that way. I preferred to jump. And I got down all right, not too far from the highway, I'll have to make it that far; they're not going to pick me up two feet outside the wall, are they?

The place and the night when I will see Rolande again are still far away: first I've got to drag this lump that keeps me from walking out to the road ... twice, three times I try to put my foot down: lightning strikes, shoots through my leg. ✦

Since my feet are useless, I will walk on my knees and elbows. I crawl twenty yards, I bump into some bushes, I get back onto the pavement, trying to orient myself.

Another century must have gone by, I can't recognize anything.

My ankle is locked, the foot and leg at right angles; I heave it along like a weight, up and down, it seesaws between the cement and the thorny bushes. The night is opaque. From up there, all these last months, I used to look down at those bushes so close to the highway and I was sure I could find my way with my eyes closed: my plans hadn't gotten that far yet, but all the same a constant temptation to jump and run away would automatically take this path. And, smiling at the shivering girls herded around the matron, squeezing Rolande's hand when she slid it into my pocket, I would fly down to the pavement and I would pick myself up, hee hee, crafty and purified....

And we would go back into the lights, dragging our feet. I would leave my friend's hand in my pocket and I would feel around inside hers to find through the material the one-two of the joint, Rolande, I can feel your bone walking.... And we would burst out laughing inside our coats, and the bright lights of the hall would drown out our dreams until the next day.

I crawl along. My elbows are covered with dirt, I am oozing mud, thorns scratch me at random from the bushes, I am in pain but I must keep going, at least as far as that light, over there, a house which must be on the highway ... between me and the light, there is an iron fence which I fall against: I feel good, here, lying on my back, my eyes closed, my arms limp.... They'll pick me up while I'm asleep, so what. I'll pay for this rest with punishments, more suffering, I was heading for the ground, that's where I'm staying. Maybe the wall will follow me down and bury me under it.

I am up, on the soles of my kneecaps, I drag myself along the fence. One knee, one elbow, one knee, one elbow... it's O.K., I'm getting used to it. I dream that I'm starting over again, that I'm taking my time: instead of hurtling down like a maniac, gripping onto the stones and letting go when my foot touches emptiness, I look for a soft place to land, a place where the grass grows thick and springy....

I pass the house, whose light is still shining; I go on along the wall, on the grassy path, elbow, knee, elbow... there is the road, gleaming, divided by the yellow line. There is a metal sign on the sidewalk advertising a brand of gas: I hang onto it, the panel clangs, I will start hitchhiking here.... No, Paris is in the other direction, let's go across. The first step is a white-hot poker, the second jelly, I pitch forward across the yellow line, the first car will run over me.... Here it comes, it's a truck: it's going my way and will take shreds of me to Paris sticking to its wheels. I stare at it, into its huge yellow eyes. It bears down on me.

A few yards off the truck veers, mounts the embankment and stops. I hear the air brakes, then the door slams and steps approach. I stay flattened out, my eyes closed.

"Miss!..."

Fingers touch me, searching, hesitant, anxious.

I say:

"If you don't mind, get me out of the road.... Hold me, I think I have a broken leg."

The truck driver helps me over to the running board of the truck. I sit down there, my ankle pulled back into the shadows. I don't want to look. A street lamp, very close, lights my right foot: it is covered with dirt, mud is drying around the black nails and rises in thick coils up to my knee, which is striped with cuts where drops of blood slowly form. I hug myself in my coat, my fists in my pockets: I don't have another stitch on and I'm getting cold, cold to my very heart.

"Could you let me have a cigarette?"

The guy gets out his Gauloises and gives me a light. In the flame I see his face, the face of truck drivers at night: the luminous skin, the stubble beginning to grow, and that worn-out, fixed expression.

"What happened to you?"

"I ... oh, what the heck. The mess I'm in, I have nothing to lose. You know this neck of the woods?"

"I make this run three times a week, I guess I do."

I point across the road to where the prison beacon is the only landmark in a confused blob of trees and walls.

"Then, you probably know what that is over there...."

"Oh.... Yes. That's where you...?"

"Yes, just this minute. Well, a hall-hour ago, an hour.... They can't be looking for me yet. Oh, please, take me to Paris. You won't get into trouble, I promise you. In Paris, just drop me off and I'll make out all right."

The man thinks, a long time, and then says:

"I'd like to help you out, but ... you understand, there's your leg."

"But even so.... Just as far as Paris, Mister, that's all I ask of you. I'll never breathe a word about you, no matter what happens. Believe me."

"I believe you. But you can't change things, 'they' have ways of finding out that we don't even know about. I've got a wife and kids, I can't."

I take my ankle in both hands and brace myself against the cab in an effort to get up:

"O.K. then, leave me. Only, please, don't tip 'them' off at your next stop. Forget about meeting me, be …"

I was about to say, "Be kind," but suddenly I realize bow meaningless those words are, just like the taste of the cigarette I've almost finished, and the ten minutes this man has given me.

"Listen," he says, "there's one thing I can do, I can flag down a car for you: a private party might take you…. I'll give them some story…."

Let him do what he wants. Me, I only want to amputate this leg and go to sleep, sleep until it grows back again and wake up laughing about my dream. Recently Cine wrote me: "My darling, I had a nightmare: you had fallen, very badly, from very high up, your ears were bleeding and there was nothing I could do for you, nothing except cry…. When I woke up I looked at your picture and almost died of joy because it wasn't true, because I was going to see you again, as you are each morning, looking like a new penny, racing off to the kitchen with your big pot of milk…."

How we laughed, Rolande and I, when we read that! Cine, last year's lover, who was still ready to drop everything for me, while I would have forgotten all about her if it hadn't been for the endless trickle of neatly folded little notes that a neutral and accommodating girl brought me almost every morning…. Cine! I was tired of her certainties, of her possessive extremes, of the mark she thought she had left on me, of her maternalism, my big girl, my little baby.

I had met Cine on a train. The men and the women were sharing a compartment in two carefully separated groups: the men were singing, the women were silent or were crying. I had plastered myself up against the window looking out at Paris, whose outlines were blurred through the triple screen of the dirty glass, the rain, and my tears, as we left it behind.

"Don't cry!..."

I sniffed up the contents of my nose as quietly as possible, ran my fingers under my eyes, and turned toward the voice. A woman of about thirty, with eyes like black olives and a brown chignon, was sitting beside me, and her smile was as pleasant as her voice. My tears stopped, and I looked at her more closely, from her soft scarf down to her slippered feet. I leaned forward a little and noticed black medium-heeled pumps under the seat—a real lady.... I asked her:

"A long time?"

"A long time ... done, or left to do?"

"Left: the rest is none of my business!"

"Oh, why not? It's no secret: seven years, in all."

"Hey, the same as me.... I've got five left, and you?"

"You never know how much you've got left: there are pardons, parole...."

"Nah," I said, "that's a lot of talk. I'm crying, yes, because I'm quite convinced that I'm leaving Paris for five years. Look, it's all over already, anyhow. If only those men would stop singing! Thank God they'll be getting off soon."

We exchanged first names and ages.

"But you're a minor! How ..." Francine said.

"I beg your pardon, I'm an adult! Criminally adult, mentally adult, completely adult. The proof is that I waited two years, like a big girl, so that they could hang five more on me. I'm young, but where we're going everyone is young. I think prison schools only take people under thirty, or thirty-five."

During the morning, the countryside changed, blurred, stripped itself bare: we were "going up" north. Around noon the train stopped, finally: I was dying to take off my shoes. I hadn't thought to get out my slippers, and, from having dragged around so long in prison shoes, I'd lost the habit of wearing high heels.

"Tie up your shoes!"

I'd heard that for two years, along with "Wipe that frown off your face" and "Go and put on your slip, naked under your sweater, no but, that's not nice, I'm telling you!..." What would they yell at me next?

"Would you like a hand?"

They weren't ordering us around anymore, they were making suggestions, and the suggestions were sung rather than barked; our troupe gathered on the platform, and smiling and seraphic women helped us carry our suitcases, our badly-tied bundles, our shopping bags stuffed with various things, all indispensable.

"Let's try to stay next to each other, all right?" Francine said,

After that, other signals, other coincidences brought us together: we were assigned to the same group, and therefore visited by the same matron during the three months of solitary. We talked over the walls of the individual exercise yards, or during chores, dishwashing, cleaning, which we also did together: two by two, in the same group, Cine and I, taking turns with the others.

After the three months, we would rejoin the same group. We spoke about that day with more excitement than about the day when we would be released, which was still too far away; we dreamed of a sort of *vita nuova*, of an obliteration of the past in the brightness and tidiness of the group, sequestered, starched … in short, young boarding-school girls, little sheep, choirs of angels singing in unison.

Cine, why did those innocent plans have to end up in a cursed reality? Instead of letting me quietly pursue my little dream, why did you have to throw mud all over it? I was taking chances, making magic, signs of the cross, because I didn't have much to get me through my youth and my boredom; you knew it, we laughed about it together, at night leaning out of the windows of our barless rooms (we weren't allowed to call them "our cells"), you sometimes scolded me … and then, you whose friendship I loved, you wanted to burden me with your love. You believed that you, you would be able to graft feelings onto me, sew a piece of your heart to me. …

At any rate, Cine was asleep, up there, and her dream was coming true: something like "my darling ears" was bleeding to death, was dying slowly, here, on the edge of the road where I would never walk again, with you, Cine, or Rolande or anyone else, because I would never walk again. From the way I was sitting on the running board of the truck, I couldn't imagine any future other than lying down, definitive immobility.

"There are never any cars, at this hour," the truck driver said, coming back. "How's it going?"

"Oh, it's not any worse than it was. Go ahead, go on, I've already held you up enough. Anyhow, they won't be long in coming to look for me. …"

The sound of an engine rose from the depths of the night: the guy sprang forward. I saw his silhouette, outlined by the headlights, gesticulating wildly. How fast the cars go, nowadays! He's going to get run over. … I leaned back in the shadow of the cab and closed my eyes. The car had stopped; a door slammed, and footsteps and voices were approaching. Dimly,

I made out a man, motionless in front of the truck driver who was talking to him, pointing at the prison wall, then at me.... The man turned his back to the streetlight and made a precise shadow, hunched over, his hands in his pockets and his collar turned up. Although they were talking quite close to me I could hardly hear a word: a fog thick as cotton and translucent as glass separated me from them, and I sank deeper and deeper into it, as into sleep.

"Could I take a look at that foot?" the silhouette said.

My swollen knee could no longer do the job of getting my leg out from under the running board; I helped it by hauling on my ankle with both hands. Then, automatically, I stepped down on my heel to stand up, and what I felt was so excruciating, so hopeless, that I gave up and let my foot slide back into the shadow and the mud.

The man knelt down in front of me and got out a flashlight; I saw the smooth blond of his hair, the rose ochre of his ear and his hand. He stood back up, turned off his flashlight and went off toward his car with the truck driver. Let them go. It didn't matter to me. Again, I had stopped listening or caring. After that, everything happened very fast.

An arm went around my shoulders, another slid under my knees, I was lifted up, carried away; the man's face of a moment ago was very close, above mine, moving across the sky and the tree branches. He carried me firmly and gently, I was out of the mud and I was moving, in his arms, between the sky and the earth. The man turned into a side road, went on a few yards, then laid me carefully down on the ground; growing used to the dark, I could make out a big tree, grass, some puddles of water.

"Don't speak to anyone and above all don't move," the man

said before getting up. "I'll be back to get you, wait for me. Give me enough time."

And he went away. A little later I heard the engines of the truck and the car, lights slid past, and then everything was silence again, emptiness, night.

I didn't move: in a while, if I had less pain, I'd get a little closer to the highway. I was too far down this side road, the man wouldn't be able to find me again. I would go back a few yards the way we had come, past a few trees. I had plenty of time: I knew that the nearest town was twenty-five miles away: twenty-five plus twenty-five.... There had been other people in the car, I'd heard them talking, maybe the man wanted to drop off his passengers before coming back: "Don't speak to anyone.... I smiled, my mouth pressed against the roots of the tree; now, I was completely stretched out, I was getting soaked through in the grass, I was freezing little by little. At the other end of me my ankle was pounding heavily, bursting into incandescent waves at each beat of my heart: I had a new heart in my leg, still irregular, responding inordinately to the other. Above, the black branches were stiff in the icy sky; on the highway, cars sped by and disappeared, not one slowed down, not one turned in toward me: the man had to come back, since I no longer had the strength to go and look for another ride, and since they mustn't find me here, in the morning. I wasn't the least bit worried about my leg, it would be taken care of somehow. Already the pain had grown familiar, it wandered through my body, visiting every recess and numbing it, it spread out and settled down; only little sudden stabs, here and there, made me jump and kept me from going to sleep altogether.

I fingered the butt of the Gauloise the truck driver had

given me in my pocket: perhaps it would be my only trophy. . . .
That wasn't so bad, after all: I had a butt, a real big Gauloise
butt, and I was free to throw it away or crumble it up. I'd left
my rolling paper and my matches up there; Rolande, Rolande,
I've got a beautiful butt and I can't smoke it. . . .

A match striking. A shooting star, a searchlight. No, it's the
forge in my ankle illuminating the whole crossroad: the sparks
whirl around for a moment, then gather and freeze into a brilliant circle of light, a huge torch whose beam passes through
the base of my head and lands, without striking me, on the
tree trunk. It also seems to me that the brief, dying sound of an
engine has swelled the night; but I must have been dreaming,
only the cold grates on my ears. All the same, the headlight
is still there, I can make out the details of the tree's bark, and
now a second one lights up, tiny and wavering, which searches
rapidly, close to the ground. It's all over, I've been found.

Everything is turned off and someone approaches. It's him,
surely.

"I thought I told you not to move!"

Oh, have I moved? It's possible. Everything is possible
again. I think I'm laughing, that I have my arms around the
man's neck, that . . .

"All right, all right," he says, freeing himself to reach into the
inside pocket of his jacket. He gets out a flat bottle and a pack of
cigarettes. We have all the time in the world now: we take turns
drinking from the bottle; at each puff the ends of our cigarettes
draw our faces out of the darkness. Finish this pack and this
bottle, and after that, who cares? I've got my hope back.

The man goes on taking out things:

"Here, I brought you a pair of pants, a sweater, there's an
Ace bandage, too. . . ."

It's true, I'm practically naked. I take off my coat and put on the sweater. But the pants ... how can I get into a pants leg with this blown up foot that won't even bend anymore, that kills me at the slightest touch? I put my coat back on and I say:

"What's your name?"

Now we are two first names, together we will leave the black trees, and in the morning we can find out the rest. But first get out of here, fast....

"You don't want to at least try to put the bandage on? It's freezing you know."

"Oh no, let's leave it alone, please. I'll go barefoot, it doesn't matter."

"If you say so. I'm going to ride you on my motorcycle, so hang on to me. Let me know if you're not O.K. You know how to ride?"

"Yes, I used to know how, don't worry. Let's get going now, come on."

I curl myself around the steady flame the alcohol has lighted in me, I let my foot hang down beside the wheel, and I grip onto Julien's shoulders with both arms.

A new century begins.

2

I had not trembled, earlier, when I opened my fingers to let go of the wall; all night I had been inert and tensed, I hadn't had time to grasp what was happening to me; but now, under the bright bulb in the kitchen, I was beginning to perceive my pain, even as I rediscovered warmth and rest, and I allowed myself to shake all over, in every bone. Propped up between the sink and the oven, I tried to control my chattering teeth and my whole body which was racked by a storm of nerves that reached down to my chair, to the cigarette I was holding. I noticed that I was wearing a man's pajama bottom and a black cable-knit sweater: the prison coat had disappeared.

I had been installed in a chair; another chair with a pillow had been slid under my legs; shadows moved before me, my savior from the night, another taller man, an old lady, very tiny. I still couldn't make out what they were saying, but I heard and smelled coffee being made: the rattle of the coffeepot, the drip of the filter, the slightly bitter odor. My foot had stopped crying out, like a dog who, after howling a long time in the night, is let into the house and goes to sleep by the fire.

The big guy was feeling my ankle, looking like a worried doctor; the old lady was bringing bandages and bottles, and heating water.

"That's my mother," Julien said.

The mother washed away my blood and covered my clean foot with an enormous bandage. Nobody seemed surprised or asked questions, their actions were relaxed and efficient. Perhaps I had come home, to the house where I grew up, after an obscure and painful journey, and this woman was my mother too. Still carried by Julien, now I was going up the stairs to the second floor, to get back into my old bed in the kids' room.

"Now try to sleep a little," Julien said, kissing me lightly on the cheek. "I'll be back in the morning. And above all, don't let anybody see you at the window."

"As if I could walk that far!..."

"That's true. There now, go to sleep. Everything will seem clearer tomorrow."

He turned out the light and closed the door, only letting one chink of light come in.

My bed, very small, the bed of a big child, was in the middle of the room; to the right and the left, against the walls, I could make out two others, these cribs, with low mattresses and bars. There were movements: little gurgles, little happy or frightened cries, sudden eruptions of covers, then a return to the deep, slightly nasal, breathing of children asleep. We were three kids, and my foot was down there at the end of me like a huge stuffed doll. Inch by inch, I had eased it to the bottom of the bed, and my right leg, bent up, made a tent for it to protect it from the weight of the sheet. I was lying inside a rectangle, with, attached to me, an unfamiliar weight that prevented my escape; a weight of extraordinary inertia and rigidity, an obstinate, dead member, a piece of living wood with no regard for me or the efforts of my head and muscles to force it to obey.

At dawn, a young woman came into the room; she was wearing a red bathrobe over her nightgown. She smiled, vaguely, opening the curtains. She didn't seem at all surprised to see me there, either. She gently shook the little bundles in the beds, murmuring: "Come on, it's time to get up now ..." and I felt like being wakened too, and going downstairs to toast and jam and schoolbags with these two pretty children, whom the red bathrobe made say, "Good morning, Miss...."

But, embarrassed both by my unusual situation—dropped in my immense pajamas into the middle of their night—and by my unfamiliarity with children, I smiled as best I could, saying good morning as though they were grownups, Miss who must be seven and Sir who was all of five, good morning. I, who had known nothing but cruelty in my childhood, what on earth was I doing here, in this cheerful nursery, with its toys and books spread all over the floor, its blue rug and its big window framing a gray spring morning?

Several days went by like that. In the morning, after the children had left for school, Ginette would come up, or the mother, with breakfast and hot water for washing; my life was reorganizing itself, elementary: I now had my own comb, my toothbrush, nightgowns, and underwear lent by Ginette; Eddie, the big guy, Ginette's husband, had brought an old radio down from the attic and plugged it in beside my bed: I listened to it all day until the children went to bed, and at night I turned my leg over inside the rectangle, overcome with insomnia, waiting for dawn.

I managed to wash without too much trouble, but for the other operations I had to learn a whole new method of procedure, calculating and inventing every move: get to the basin on the floor without stepping on my left foot, bend over with lay leg held up with one hand—I had to hold it for it was completely immobilized from the knee down—maneuver back Into the bed, empty the water into the bucket.... Most of the I time I left my foot under the covers, and I moved by starting from the knee, rolling from side to side, crawling in place, leaning on my shoulders.

All the same, I took stock of the situation every morning, by trying to walk. Seated on the edge of the bed, I would put my foot down, I would stand up; gradually I would distribute my weight, I would bear down equally on both legs: after a few streaks the pain would settle into a large motionless ball, subside. Then I would activate my right foot, curling it, lifting it off the floor, carefully, slowly.... But I always got going too fast, my knee would get away from me, buckle, and I would be thrown backwards onto the bed or forward to the floor. Beaten until the next day, I would pick up my leg again and once more lay it out horizontally.

I would also take off the bandage, to look at it: during the first days the calf and ankle looked as though they'd been in a prize fight, the foot was the base of a cone and the swelling had obscured the ankle. Blue, purple, and green blotches of blood stagnated under the skin, and the bramble scratches traced a network of black crusts across the surface; every now and then I would come across a pricker and pull it out with my fingernails. Then the swelling went down: the wood turned to hard, cold marble, the blood no longer circulated.

By day, the little romantic novels Ginette brought me, the simple tunes on the radio, and the half-empty bottles Eddie would bring me asking me to finish them kept the beast from showing its teeth; and also, they would come to see me, sitting carefully on the edge of my rectangle, and their presence, their conversation would pass the time. Ginette vacuumed and made the beds, humming to herself, answering the questions I asked out of politeness, with difficulty, for one fear was always with me: I had the impression that everything I said, and even my silences, revealed a fact I was not ashamed of, no, but that I couldn't very well shout from the rooftops either. I had learned to love girls, to gauge them, I had been steering clear of mothers barricaded behind their kids to try and hide their extramarital affairs and their crimes; the women I had left up there behind the wall had turned me away from simplicity, from even the most superficial friendship, and the gap between them and Ginette stupefied and silenced me.

To Julien, on the other hand, I had told everything: the past, the future that I was sure of, to walk, to walk and then to find Rolande again. He had come back two nights after rescuing me: recognizing his voice downstairs, I had been surprised, even irritated, that he didn't come up to see me right away.

"My mother says it's all right," he had explained when he came back to get me that night in the black trees. And:

"Don't screw things up and get her into trouble."

He was coming to see his mother, and I was getting restless.

Later, long after Eddie and Ginette had gone to bed, Julien opened the door; he moved like a ghost, not turning on the lights, not bumping into anything. When he got close to me he shone a flashlight shielded by his fingers onto the bed, and sat down.

I could only see the bulk of his silhouette and two lighted hands: I took one of them and felt up his bare arm, stopping at a pajama sleeve rolled up over a hard bicep, hard.... Four years without touching a man's arm.

"Do you like white rum?"

I had never tasted it, but I said yes, anyhow.

In the darkness of the room, broken by the soft beam of the flashlight on the bedside table, we could hardly see each other, and we spoke very quietly so as not to wake the children.

All those four years, the night would keep bringing me the same dream: a shape, a voice, a presence: a man whom I pushed away angrily by day after calling to him at night; a very large shadow, very protective, who sometimes called me "lonely little puppy," a voice that always understood me.

"The things we don't dream about, I swear!"

And we would laugh, under the intrigued or indignant eyes of good wives and mothers.

"Three out of five were there for infanticide," I explained to Julien. "So, since three-fourths of the rest were just old bags, that left a little group of us, a very little group. During the three months of solitary you knit underwear for supply, you make samples of stitches on pieces of cloth which they paste into a notebook: that way they can classify the girls according to what they know how to do. You're weighed, measured, tested … then you're assigned to a group. It was against the rules for one group to communicate with another: each one had its own dining room, recreation room, and its own matron. It was stupid, since we were all mixed together in the workshops, and it's mostly during the day that you talk and get to know each other.… You can imagine the deals that went on between groups, all the girls at their windows at night screaming and calling to each other, the note-passing, etc. My cell was next to Cine's. In the morning the matron would unbolt the doors ("Good morning, Anne, did you sleep well?" and me: "Oh yes, Miss!"), then she would hole up in the kitchen, downstairs. Cine would come and help me get up … you know what I mean.... On top of that we had to be ready to go down to breakfast with the others: some rat race. Or else I would go and wake up Cine; but that bothered me. Her bookcase—because we had little bookcases, above the upholstered beds, I guess you'd call them studio couches—her bookcase was full of pictures of her husband and kids. I liked my joint better, one of the few with no man and no kids. We used to get together in my room with the other members of the gang ... anyhow, everything was fine until the day that dirty-assed business got mixed up in it."

"Me, when I was up at Central...." Julien said.

I knew it: "Don't talk to anybody," the furtive walk, like the profile, the complete and mysterious affinity between us from the very start.... Ginette had indeed told me that her brother was a "tough guy," but I'd seen in that a kind of sympathy to me who'd been in Central ... long before he said anything, I had recognized Julien. There are certain signs imperceptible to people who haven't done time: a way of talking without moving the lips while the eyes, to throw you off, express indifference or the opposite thing; the cigarette held in the crook of the palm, the waiting for night to act or just to talk, after the uneasy silence of the day.

The rum was disappearing in the bottle; night was turning into dawn, rustling. With Julien sitting and me lying down, it was easy and natural for me to rest my head on his chest, to let myself be held, rolled into a ball from my knees up, my pain stored away somewhere else. I said:

"I hate men. No, not even that, I've forgotten them. Look, Julien, when I'm stroking your chest how my hands curve around you, how hard you seem to me, how weak I feel...."

Julien was calling me back to man.

Marveling, I kept saying: "Stay, stay ..."

"I've got to go downstairs now. Because of my mother: I sleep in her room, and ..."

"Oh, stay ..."

"A few minutes, then."

"I won't go to sleep. I'll be calling you."

Since my fall, I couldn't remember having slept. Sometimes, the unconsciousness of night must have slid into that of sleep, of course, but without ever stopping the flow of images and the steady hammer of the flesh, now well established in its new state. Circuits had been formed, cadences: in my ankle, suddenly, something would wake up hissing, like water spurting from a broken pipe, more springs would start gushing, then they all would run together and flow insidiously through the length of my body. Or else, the pain would gather into a ball above my heel, slowly twisting and winding itself up; when the ball was finished—I now could tell the exact moment—it would burst with a sensation of light; and the flashes would shoot through my foot and explode, in stars that quickly went out, in the ends of my toes. Then, I could relax: it would be a while before the next ball formed. I had never had a fracture; but I knew there was a stew of shattered bones and flesh inside there, and that a great deal of art and patience would be needed to put it back in order. Unless ...

I was lying pressed against the edge of the little bed so that Julien could stretch out on his back; I was leaning on my elbows, my face above his, in the darkness: the flashlight had gone out, nothing was left of it but a little round, reddish eye, far away from us. With my stomach against Julien's hip, overcome with love, the rum, and the mystery of this night, I was crying out, but without real tears:

"I don't want them to ..."

Julien must have opened one eye:

"What's the trouble, my little rabbit?"

"They're going to cut off my foot.... I don't want them to! I ... But can't you see that it's rotting away my whole leg? They'll cut it off, I'll never walk again...."

But what more could I expect? Julien had saved my whole self, he would certainly save this leg too. I knew he would find the solution at the exact limit of the danger. Wait. Don't scream, grit your teeth, there is the mother, there are the kids—never surprised to see me always in bed, when they got up, at night, between the two of them; good morning, Miss, good night, chirps and laughter exchanged over my bed, but no questions, no unkindnesses ... beyond what hadn't been said to them, beyond their innocence, their eyes understood and reflected my own. I wanted to hide from them only that disgusting part of me: that smashed, battered, horrible leg.

"In a few days," Julien was saying. "Come on, just a little more courage. I'm looking for a hideout, some place where they'll take proper care of you. But it's still too close, both in distance and in time. You know they're looking all over, even in the hospitals."

And he left, and he came back a few nights later, and then again the daylight eclipsed him.

I had given up wondering and asking questions. I received the bread and water, the words and music, with the sensation of being cut off from time and from myself. There, as elsewhere, a routine had been established: shh-shh, watch out the ball is about to explode, bang, crash the kids are back from school, soon Eddie will bring me something to drink; and I will drink it, all, to quiet my pain until tomorrow, until the smell of toast comes up to me with the coffeepot and the big bowl.

Two more weeks went by. I had escaped near Easter, and nothing was rising from the dead, nothing was dying or living. I still had several months to get ready to meet Rolande; I had talked to Julien about her, and he would laugh like a fool after we made love:

"Of course, it's not quite the same with your girl friends...."
And:

"Don't worry, you'll get there: I'll carry you there if I have to."

"Can you picture it, with me on crutches!"

"We'll take you in a car, yes.... But I tell you that in two months you'll be able to run away like a rabbit. Think what you like," he added, bumping his forehead against mine, "but, above all, think that you don't owe me a thing. And that I am a son of a bitch to have slept with you."

"But Julien, you didn't rape me.... And besides, what does it matter? Aren't you mainly my brother?"

"Your brother!... Ah, if I had come to get you, and you had gotten well again, and then later, in complete freedom ... then, it would have been beautiful. But ..."

Easter bells were ringing in through the window, half-opened onto a balmy April; we were talking, glasses in our hands: for once Julien had come early and brought me up a drink. Smells of roasting meats and cakes wafted up the stairs, I felt like eating and drinking, and getting out of my rectangle. And, at that very instant, Julien asked me if I wanted to dine with the family, to give me a change from eating from a tray.

"Yes, but ... I haven't got any clothes...."

"Wait, I'll go and see if Ginette has something to lend you."

So I got ready: an old skirt and sweater, some vaseline to soften my dried out face, the one slipper on the one foot, Julien carried me to the table, which had been set in the kitchen, and sat me down between the mother and himself. The table was round and small: I moved my chair so I could put my bandaged foot on Julien's knee. During the whole meal he ate with one hand, holding my doll with the other, squeezing it a little to make it hurt less. Sitting down, the pain was different: the bones formed a vice which tightened itself, a big cube of iron clamping shut, set wrong. All the same, I laughed and ate with the others: at Easter, one foot, even that one, shouldn't be allowed to spoil everything; my foot was under the table with the other healthy feet, and it was healing from being among them.

At dessert, the little boy, gravely and without choking himself, smoked Eddie's cigar; Eddie had taken the mother onto his lap and was hugging her with one arm, with the other pulling at Ginette who was a little drunk and talking and laughing herself to death. Some chicken bones and three spoonfuls of peas were left on the platter, and the cake was waiting amid the remains, the glasses, the cast-off napkins. I was still hungry: this feast had been my first in years. Eating had become a habit and an attitude, a pastime and a pretext. I had been excused from evening classes, which didn't go above high school level: while the other girls were "at school" with the matrons, I would fix the evening meal.

I had been quick to master the course in homemaking: in fifteen minutes chow would be ready, and I would be left with a full hour and a half of freedom. I would sneak out by the kitchen window to catch a breath of fresh air on the walls, or to meet a girl who'd gotten herself excused from school for some imaginary ailment. We'd have ourselves a ball.

Yes: to be in the kitchen when the matron wasn't there, to run off upstairs when she came and lifted the lids off the pots:

"Anne, it smells delicious! What are you serving us?..."

On Sundays, the matron sat at the table with her flock. We would have danced a little, after mass we wrote to our families, and now we stuffed ourselves with Anne's good grub. The walk, in a little while, would help us to digest. We drag our feet, your small bone walking—walk faster, my darling bone!—our bellies heavy with dough, on to dinner when we'll stuff some more, until we get sleepy, *ouf*, and fall asleep, another week done.

Holy Grail: the butter rolls stolen from the commissary, the chickens killed in the lower yard just before inventory every three months, cooked, divided up and eaten on the sly; the birthday packages for the girls on welfare, obligatorily deposited in the collective pool. Thanks, Mom, from what they tell me your pigeons were very good. My darling, bring up your ball of string tonight, I'll lower something to you out of the window, you'll have a feast. That's right, Miss, my quart of milk is never full, I'm being robbed, I work, I need my milk.

The Grail, litany, blues, gravy spots. Even the "*apéritif*," violated weeks before the feast days we observed, never warmed me like this wine here outside: I'm looped.... The desire to lie down, to float, mounted in me in waves of well-being; I pressed my heel against Julien's pants, come on, let's go upstairs, drop this family conversation which drags on and on and doesn't include me.

With all the gravity of drunkenness, they solemnly escorted me upstairs and formed a circle around my leg, unwrapped it, and applied their fingers, one by one, trying to make it bend and move. At this, I let myself go and cried: it was true, it was a glaring truth, my foot was a menace to all of us. Not even Julien could comfort me; he only turned my tears into rage, get me out of here, take me anywhere, bring me back if you want, the important thing is my leg and soon it will be too late to save it.

Julien promised: tomorrow.

"... and try not to make a pass at the guy with the car, he's my buddy."

Where had Julien my lover gone? Why was he making a fool of me, why was he being cruel? Why was he destroying our tenderness? Did he think that my loving him had been part of a deal, that I'd been paying it off, when all I was trying to do, still, was to get better and find my pride again?

... One morning, finally, a car pulled up in front of the house. Ginette had helped me climb into a pair of her slacks and stuff the contents of the night table into a beach bag. I was a little richer, richer in underwear, in soap and sleeping pills. These had been prescribed, along with compresses of saline solution and saltwater baths, by the family G.P. who'd been called in one night when I'd been thrashing around terribly: "a massive sprain," he had diagnosed.

Well, let's get going for this sprain, then, even though it's nothing like the sprains of my childhood, which never stopped me from running around for long and promised, beneath the slight discoloration and the good pain, to heal quickly. War wound or not, it's still a sprain: I'll surprise them, I'll go downstairs by myself, I ... ow, here I am on the floor again, I couldn't make it. Quick, one knee, one elbow, my foot held up, climb back into my rectangle, don't let them find me sprawled out here.

"Hello, you're ready? Good. I'll carry you down."

Julien came in like a whirlwind, kissed me without looking at me, put his arm under my knees, hung the beach bag over his shoulder. And I, with my arms around his neck in a now-familiar pose, I looked at my rectangle with its sheets in disorder, the basin full of soapy water, the beds where the kids were still sleeping; a ray of sunshine slanted in through the closed shutters:

"It's a nice day?" I asked.

"Hot, even. There's going to be a lot of traffic, it's the first of May."

Introductions. Cordiality, coffee, embraces. I discerned, in the general good humor, a hint of relief: I was going to be taken care of, but also I was going to be somewhere else.... During these three weeks, my hosts had perhaps, also, found the time long.

There was no danger of the police coming to get me there, of course; but they might have dropped in looking for Julien, who was not supposed to be in that district and had picked me up on his way through.

"You think I'm going to let them keep me from seeing my mother!"

That's why he came at night, when the police don't knock at quiet houses, and left before dawn. I was hidden up on the second floor; if they had come, by chance or on a tip from some kind neighbor, they wouldn't have had a search warrant, and Ginette and the mother could have let them in, wide-eyed, inviting them to look around; and even if ... well, a cousin of theirs could always have broken her leg. But the deathblow mocks our best laid plans, and the little push that derails the train is often caused by an excess of zeal, on one side or another.

The friend was very fat, very jolly, about fifty, well turned out: the image I'd formed of a hood who'd made it, retired from prison and business.... I was bursting with images anyhow: I'd been locked up too young to have seen much of anything, and I'd read a lot, dreamed and lost the thread. For me, reality was distorted like everything else; and, while they were settling me in the backseat—I could stretch out completely—I pictured myself heading for some luxurious, frightful den of iniquity.

The road was all innocent, springlike, jammed with cars loaded with families, blossoming with little stands selling bellflowers: the road of the lily of the valley.

Julien was chatting with his friend. I could see his ears neatly outlined by the cut of his blond hair, his neck, a little white collar showing above the navy blue suit: blue, blond, shaved, rosy, and the other blue, shaved, rosy, and graying. My fate from now on was to go from a bed to a car seat, from a car seat to a bed, to be put down, lugged around at will by friendly men and strangers, who owed me nothing and from whom I had to borrow.

And, far from being embarrassed, I felt frustrated, sulky, I made unspoken demands: everything is my due, but I want to take it for myself. I can no longer take, and I do not know, I must not try to find out what it is that I'll be given.

We were so happy, darling, those last nights ... that bed you had given me, I could at least do you its honors; hiding my astonished feelings under the easy parade of gestures, I was at once a virgin and an expert.... But now we have left, the back of that seat is thicker than the wall that wounded me, the doors are locked; and I can only find, in the gentle rocking of the car rolling on and on, impressions from before what has been, recently, my life. A life had taken shape, after my arrest: for years, I had let it sprout, joyously absurd, naive and shameless.

In that life, you were never carried off, petted, saved; you stood up straight, in the dark cages of the paddy wagon, or sat up on the hard wooden slats. But in that life, all the same, you could get your kicks in secret in the certainty of each day's routine. My new freedom imprisons me and paralyzes me.

3

"Come on, Nini, don't make that awful face. Open us up a bottle instead."

"Oh sure, now he's in a good mood, now that he's dropped his package off here!..."

Nini is dark-skinned, thin and bony, with a flat chest, sharp, high-colored cheek bones, small bright eyes. All her femininity comes from her accessories: little curls, a tight dress, thick but high heels. She looks like a marionette, she must be a Jordanian. From what I could gather, she used to be a servant here before buddying up with the owner, and the owner's mother and his son.

The driver, who has accepted a drink—"just a taste, my wife's expecting me"—Julien, who has changed from his shoes in an old pair of slippers, Nini, Pierre her man, and finally me, "the package!": we're alone in the roadhouse. Not a customer, not another sign of life or greeting of the trade: since closing, Pierre has banished the smile and the backslap and the rest of it to some place under the dust of the abandoned décor.

The dining room, rustic, sunny, opens into the bar through a widely arched doorway whose curtains are kept open: I can see the dirty counter, the disordered shelves, empty bottles and old telephone books side by side with a basket of laundry and an iron, piles of old papers, notebooks, sheet music.... I wonder if he's letting the place go to pot from spite at having had to close it, or in the hope of opening up again any day. In the latter case, lied just have to arrange the tables and dust a little.

There emanates from all this bric-a-brac a mixture of artificial good cheer and sadness; and I, used to the narrowness of cells, feel a little dizzy in the presence of all this space: the dance floor next to the bar, no longer waxed and gleaming, the bandstand with the instruments embalmed in their black cases, leaning against the piano or against the stacks of chairs.

A window above the dance floor illuminates and details every surface with the precision of a floodlight. Where we're sitting, the sun enters, more softly, through the bay window in the dining room, and with it all the greenness of the terrace: pots and jars of all sizes, holding all kinds of plants and flowers, have replaced the little tables where you used to drink outdoors; down below, the gate, the path, the river.

I ask, just to say something:

"Do you swim here? I guess, when you live ten yards from the water, your first thought in the morning must be to take a dip."

"In all that slime!" Pierre says. "At least, it's good for the shrimp. And then, it attracts customers: a little accordion music, a little canoeing...."

Not deigning to continue, he gets up to unhook his old accordion and starts absentmindedly fingering a few chords, letting the bellows wheeze slowly. He appears to be very hot: his fat torso is clad only in an undershirt, and I can see his damp armpits, his glistening forehead.

"Do you know music?"

I try to give him my references: years of violin lessons in a provincial conservatory, scales and fingering rusty from lack of practice, but that ...

"Hey, Julien," Pierre interrupts me, putting down his beat-up box to pick up his glass—one quart water, two drops pastis, a pale cloudy drink for a retired lush—"when you can work it, bring her a violin, she could saw away on it all day! And by the way, when you get an amplifier, remember me, huh? And the Solex for Nini ..."

Julien says, "O.K., O.K.," comfortably settled in his chair, his legs stretched out.

I realize that my hosts feel a greedy sort of servility toward him, hidden under their friendly tone of complicity, poised between the two extremes of respect for the guy who knows how to steal, and condescension for the guy you're doing a favor for. Because, after all, they are taking me in, and with a fairly good idea of why: without going into details, Julien described me as "a runaway minor": whether I'd run away from a prison or from my parents, I still represent a risk to them. At any rate, Pierre insists on this last point, sliding over payoffs already made and yet to be made, facing up squarely to the day when I will be recaptured and when, called down to dinner ... I object:

"But you know, that was four years ago, when the cops ..."

"Aha!" Pierre jumps with joy. "See what I mean? Now, let's get one thing straight right off: I've got my kid here, and I won't permit any talk in front of him about ..."

"But he *isn't* here!"

"When he is here, it will be the same thing. You might as well get used to it right now: no 'cops,' no 'prison,' never use those words. Understand?"

O.K., but it's like being back in the clink again!

Actually, I prefer this to an interrogation. I decide, on the spot, never to say a word that isn't absolutely necessary, to be as dumb as I am immobilized, to let my leg do the howling.

To rise from the status of servant to that of mistress, Nini least have made good use of her talents as a cook: the chicken melts in your mouth, the ice cream doesn't melt in the bowl, and the cake is moist and soft. The owners wash all this down with large glasses of mineral water; Julien refills my glass and his: for the price, we do have a right to the best minerals.

Under the table, there's a supporting crossbar; I've sneaked my leg up on it, I've wedged it into the position where it hurts the least, where the explosions in my toes are least frequent.

Anyhow, the explosion doesn't even hurt anymore: there is one intense, predictable second, when all I have to do is collect myself and secretly clench my jaws, keeping my lips parted in a smile and my eyes straight ahead. In this way, my appearance bears out the general diagnosis "a bad sprain, but in a few weeks ..."

Julien, aren't you ever going to get us up? I've had too much to eat and drink, I want to sleep. I would like to talk, be a worthy guest, win back these people somehow, even though I already feel that nothing will ever bring us together and make us understand each other; they are the drop, I am the hot item: only normal that we'd want to be rid of each other in a hurry. But only my foot can tell what they've gotten themselves in for....

"Sleepy, baby?" Julien whispers.

"Not very, only whew …"

Since the beginning of the meal, I've reminded myself of a kid jiggling about shyly on a grownup's chair: I dream of rising discreetly and with dignity, saying, "Excuse me a moment," and of walking, casually, as though there were no particular hurry, to the back of the ballroom where the corner "Toilet" has lost its neon but kept the letters.

Of course Julien looks very indulgent, carrying me there.

"Can you make it, by yourself?"

"Don't worry, I won't fall in."

That's almost what happens, however, in that Turkish style bathroom with me hopping on one foot. My fingers slip on the white tiled wall, the shoe heel doesn't give me much support, the slacks bind me around my thighs.

"Julien," I say, relacing my fingers behind his neck, "now what are we going to do?"

"Be patient, we'll go take a nap in five minutes, after we have some coffee. What can you expect, that's the way they are, you'll just have to grin and bear it. But you won't have to bother with them; your meals will be brought up to you, you'll have a radio, you can take it easy: a room all to yourself. Before, you know, they had a sort of hotel here, too. …"

"And they still keep it up on the quiet, for a fat price? O.K., I get the picture. You can take me back to the table, I won't bat an eyelash."

Finally, after the interminable coffee, and a shot, and another shot, I get carried over the threshold of my new pad like a bride. A second-rate hotel room: armchair scuffed up but roomy, radiator and sink both without hot water, the inevitable discord between the flowers on the upholstery and those on the bedspread; and the mirror, always too high up, and the spotted and yellowed sheets of newspaper on the closet shelves. I stow my belongings, spreading them out as much as possible: in the daylight, Ginette's old pants lack glory, but the point is to fill up space.

I put my smokes and matches on the chair, near the head of the bed; and, quietly, I get undressed. Julien, after turning the key in the lock, has stretched out in his shirt sleeves and gone right to sleep. I've already noticed in him this ability to pass instantly from wakefulness into sleep; when he felt like sharing my rectangle, he would say good night to me and be asleep before I could answer him. Then I would amuse myself by exploring, with my fingertips, that body I had never really seen clearly and that had just been, a few seconds earlier, mine. What a small thing that was after all, what a small mark it left on our solitudes!

I would lean my hand on his chest and ask him questions, in a low voice: sometimes a conversation would begin, or else Julien was dreaming out loud, and I would bend down, attentive, oppressed by the enormous wastes of the unknown stretching between us.

One night, he said:

"I can see you.... You are wearing a smock with blue and white checks, you are running on the grass...."

In prison, the weekday uniform was a smock, with checks, blue and white. Julien had obviously never seen it, and I hadn't told him about it either.

"But," I said to the sleeper, "you've never seen me running. ..."

When he woke up, Julien had laughed like a fool:

"You're the one who was dreaming...."

I no longer tried to understand: either I would be walking

very soon, and very soon I would leave again for the dreams I left behind the wall, keeping, of these weeks, only the memory of mystery and of ineffable tenderness, an impression which I would not define, and I would go back to the girl I liked and build days and nights with her; boredom would follow, perhaps, and the dreary breakup; but the pictures would stay glued in the album of little adventures and would lead to new ones.... Or else.... Or else, I would walk for a long time to come in Julien's arms, we would make love or we wouldn't make love anymore, it wouldn't matter, but the thread woven from him to me the night of the black trees would go on strengthening and coiling itself, him, me, him, me....

Oh no! Life would manage to break it, this thread, like all the others.

For the first time, I have no desire to know the end, or even what happens next, in the story. I am here, naked, on the chair, looking at Julien who is sleeping; I would like to stay like this, lazy, warm, in the silence where only our regular breathing can be heard, without ever having to make gestures, speak words which sell us out and betray us; this moment is real and alive, I stretch it into eternity....

Then, time resumes, questions and desires nag at me again; I get up, hanging on to the closet, to cross the two huge yards that separate the chair from the bed. I cover the first yard holding my right foot out to one side, heel-toe, heel-toe, the bebop of a Saturday dance, there — and from there I dive, arms outstretched, to get a grip on the end of the bed. I drag myself up to the pillow: from very close, I study the details, pore by pore, of this face of a dead-tired man! I would like to be cruel and I want to be gentle, I'm jealous: wake up, or fix it so that I can come into your sleep too.

We go back downstairs for dinner. The hour approaches when I will be carried up, tucked in, kissed and left alone: Julien has to leave, go back to the city where he makes it look as though he had a job. He'll come back "very soon, very soon...." I have a vague desire to scream, I drip trails of egg on Ginette's sweater, and what an idea too, Nini, fried eggs, your eggs are gluey, I hate them, I'm not hungry. Julien, don't leave right away, let me pass out first. I simper:

"Could I please have a little more of that excellent brandy?"

"But ... you certainly seem to enjoy your liquor!" Pierre says, frowning. Tonight, his kid's there and he's playing the fatherly role for both our benefits. A sorry package, me: crippled, dumb, badly dressed, and a drunk. I tighten my fingers around the glass: brandy, my best buddy, my healer, my sleep. Julien takes the bottle and carries it along with me up to my room. He puts it where I can reach it; soon, I don't see him anymore, I don't see another thing until the next day.

Another week went by. After the green and gold euphoria or the trip, little by little, I grew cold again. May continued to be chilly, and the room felt damp. I camped there, wrapped up in a suede jacket that belongs to everyone: to Julien, his buddies, me, whoever needed it. I didn't dare stay in bed: the first evening, after a solitary and sleepy day, Nini had brought me up a nice meal on a tray, plenty for three hungry girls. Me, not used to eating, I'd tripled my volume and cleaned it all up. The next morning, Nini brought me fresh toast and jam arranged in a circle around a big bowl of *café au lait*; at the same time as she rang out with a professionally cheery, "Well now, did we sleep well?" she turned on the radio, opened the window.

I ate it all to the sound of music, and fell asleep again.

But, during the afternoon, Pierre came up, empty-handed:

"So, you don't want any lunch?"

"But . . . that one meal is enough for me; it's what I was used to, for several years: I can easily get back in the habit. . . . No, thank you, I can wait for the tray."

"Listen, that's all very lovely, but my wife isn't some kind of maid. . . ."

(That's true, one can't be one and have been one.)

". . . and I think that you could come downstairs and eat with us. I'll carry you."

The tray of the night before, loaded though it was, was nevertheless lighter than me. But, so as not to strain his logic, I said to Pierre that I could perfectly well get down by myself to partake of the meal served at the family table.

Now, as soon as I'd gulped down my breakfast, I'd bebop over to the sink, I'd wash all over in the glacial water, I'd get dressed; then, plunked down in the middle of the bed that I'd more or less made, my leg frozen into a painful rigidity, I'd drool over old magazines, soap operas and cigarettes, waiting for noon. At five to twelve, I'd go downstairs on my rear end, limp through the bar—progress: now I could bend my knee without using my hands—and I'd make it to the kitchen. No question of eating in the dining room: every crumb of that first feast had been swept up and digested long ago.

Pierre's mother, silent and quite dotty; Pierre, wolfing down quantities of "dietetic" food (pounds of salad, giant steaks and quarts of mineral water); Nini who ate standing up watching over the progress of the meal by the stove, all this created an uncomfortably segregated atmosphere, where eating became the only obligation of immediate value to me. Oh, of course, someday I would laugh about all these gripes; but in the meantime, I had to walk; their memory could provide vast and stimulating raw material for jokes later on; but first I had to rebuild my bones, so I had to eat, and wordlessly swallow down the calcium Nini served up in the form of cream soups thickened with vermicelli.

"It's good for you," she would say.

The calcium built up; so did the ill will. And my fracture … oh but, after all this time, it must have solidified. Even in this grotesque position, my bone must have knit, therefore it had to support me, even if it might grate a little. Furthermore, I was sick of Pierre's spoutings—"In life, you must never let yourself get flabby," he would announce, his eyes compellingly aimed at the wall above my head—I was sick of magazines and calcium soups.

Nini had given me a man's wool sock which I'd put on over the Ace bandage to try and warm my toes, purple and cold, dead; she heated basins full of hot water, added salt and invited me to soak my foot after lunch, not so much out of concern as to get me out of my room so she could vacuum; but my foot did not come alive.

The seventh morning, I missed a step and fell down the stairs, seeing stars. To get back up again was no longer a question of life or death: I didn't try. Nini found me there, my hands clenched over my ankle and my eyelids over my tears.

"But why didn't you call? Are you in pain?"

I hiccupped yes, that I couldn't stand it any longer, oh Nini, do something, my leg is dying.

"Julien called," she said, "he thinks he'll get here sometime today. But we're not going to wait for him. You can't go on like that: me, I'm calling an ambulance. Come on now, up we go, lean on me, you're going to lie down and not budge. I'll fix it up with Pierre. Pierre was, in his own words, "playing the sucker at the factory," so we had two hours ahead of us. I pretended to get hysterical:

"But that's terribly dangerous! And what name can I give, at the hospital? I don't have any identification...."

"You'll be my sister," Nini said. "I'm the one who's responsible for you, I raised you: O.K.? Don't forget ... don't forget to act like my sister in front of the nurses. All right, now, cheer up: I'll call right away."

I was getting my things together again when there came a tapping at the door: a soft scratching sound, made with the fingernails.

"Come in, Julien," I said, quite sure that I wasn't mistaken: Nini rapped on the door with her knuckles, Pierre turned the handle and walked right in; anyhow, Pierre ... he was playing the sucker: I play the sucker, but I'm not one; I too, Julien, I could get burned, but I've got a wife and kids, etc....

Before the ambulance came, we had time to make love.

4

"Have you eaten?" the nurse asks.

"Yes, two pieces of toast and some coffee and milk."

Eat, eat! Its always a question of eating. Are they going to take care of me, yes or no? I add:

"... and I'm not hungry at all."

"That's good, because you're not supposed to have anything more: they're going to premedicate you in an hour."

"They're going to what?"

"Get you ready for the table, if you prefer. In the meantime, I'm going to shave your leg."

The nurse is tiny, very young: her voice is sweet, reassuring; she sings the barbarous jargon as she manipulates the razor, with the application of a still fresh science and compassion. She touches me so much that I would like her to shave me all over: at last my leg is being taken seriously. I have even gone from one extreme to the other and start hoping that it isn't too, too serious.

The attendants had carried me from my bed to the ambulance in a wheelchair which they put down with a cautious, muffled shock like that of a luxury elevator: bump, the ground received me like thirty-six thousand layers of velvet. They put me on the emergency x-ray table, one of the attendants carrying my body, the other my leg. Nini, straight as a broomstick, her lips pursed and looking severe, forced herself to hold my hand; oh, big sister, how unfeeling your hand is, drop this farce. The admissions desk has taken your statement, your presence is no longer needed, go away.

No: she latched on to one of the men in white and succeeded in putting on an anguished tone:

"Oh, Doctor, is it serious? You won't have to keep her here, will you?"

I sat up part way and listened, leaning on my elbows, my foot exposed to the harsh light.

"Yes, I'm afraid we will, Madame: it's a bad fracture, the astragalus, the entire ankle ..."

The doctor noticed that I was watching his lips and left the room, taking Nini with him. How long would I have to stay on this new metallic, inhuman rectangle? The incomprehensible décor, bizarre, geometric, full of levers, boxes, tubes, rattles and purrs, the peaceful warmth, slightly damp, worried me and soothed me at the same time. I had come to a new point of departure, and already an opaque barrier had been erected between the morning and the present moment: the hard table melted beneath me into a safe harbor, I caught my breath and began to hope again.

Nini came back, alone. Her severe look had given way to an air of gravity:

"You know, you might lose it...."

I didn't ask what. The silence began to howl, a wedge of screams blocked my throat; I looked at my foot, black and ghastly, my foot which would be thrown into the garbage can. And suddenly I realized how much each cell, each drop of my blood meant to me, how much I was cell and blood, multiplied and divided to infinity in the whole of my body: I would die if I had to, but all in one piece.

On the other hand, these ideas of death, of amputation, remained distant, exterior, even a little burlesque: on top of the wall too, before loosening my grip, I had thought "you're going to be a dead duck," but without really believing it. Here again, the threat seemed deferred, reaching me through stories and images lived by others; the life which pulsed in me, the very recent memories of jumping and running about, the love remembered from the morning, kept me within the bounds of reality.

Reality, that putrefaction? . . . It belonged only to me, in any case. I had rejected it, long before the doctors, but I refused them the right to do as much: I took back my putrefaction and one of two things would have to happen, I would save it or I would putrefy with it.

The ward: only six beds, four of them occupied.

I indicated the one furthest from the door and nearest the bathroom:

"Can I have that one?"

Of course. No more package, no more drag, no more freakishness: in this room it was Nini and the other healthy people who seemed out of place; I fell into line, fitted in, I became "the patient in number five," and it seemed quite natural that I had a black leg. My leg justified my presence, earned me solicitude and smiles, it was a beautiful fracture, quite an accomplishment, in the end.

The sun warms my foot through the sheet. Since my fall, I have never been as warm as I am this afternoon. When I had been drinking or Julien had been making love to me, a glow would run through me but cool right away, and a blanket of cold enveloped me all the time. Here, the rays warm me more and more, also, the radiators work, the boiler turned low: I feel at ease, I don't even feel pain anymore.

My bed is strange: on the mattress there is a bottom sheet covering the bolster, on which another is folded in half and tucked in as a draw sheet; over me, a sheet, a blanket, another sheet striped with the hospital monogram in blue thread: like a compress. I have two pillows, but if I want three, or four, or ten, all I have to do is ask....

I roll over toward the night stand, with two shelves, on my right, to get my cigarettes. After the first puff, the bed across from me, perpendicular to mine, comes to life: a young woman is lying in it flat on her back, only her arms move. A mirror is fastened above her head, which she works with a pulley system: in this way she can see what's happening in the room without moving her head. It can't be much fun to have to stare at yourself all day in the ceiling like that. The girl adjusts her view-finder, she's looking for me. She speaks, her eyes fastened on my image:

"Be careful that the floor nurse doesn't see you, it's against the rules ... especially if you're going to the operating room! ..."

"Oh, I'm sorry," I say, "I didn't know...."

"It's not that it bothers us, I smoke too and the other patients don't mind. But it's better to wait until visiting hours. And today, it could make you sick, 'afterwards' ..."

"When are the visiting hours?"

"From noon till two, and at night from six to seven, Sundays all afternoon. I don't want to be indiscreet, but ... is that your mother, the dark-haired lady who was with you? She looks like you."

"She's my older sister," I say solemnly. "But I think of her as a mother, she brought me up."

Not knowing exactly whether I'm an orphan, or saddled with parents who are sick, or far away, I decide to wait until my sister gives me the details of my family situation, so that I can relay them with assurance. At the admissions desk, I had given my real first name and my correct age: the first name because I like it, and the age because I'm afraid the doctors would guess it anyhow from the state of my bone structure: I haven't grown for half a dozen years; but I had been precocious, I could be arrested; and I still have several hours to go before the cartilage is fully developed.

Will Nini come back this evening? Julien promised me he would telephone her during the afternoon. Between him and me there are only messages that can't be communicated by telephone, but I hope all the same, I don't know exactly what ... later, when I can walk, that our walk together will seem normal, a guy holding the arm or the hand of a girl in the street ... I will get to know streets with Julien, I will learn where they lead.... I bury my face in the pillows and close my eyes. The other patients are resting too, in the weird cocoon of their beds deformed by blanket hoops, from the toot of some of which emerges a cord passing over a pulley and supporting a weight. They are immobile, their eyes focused on a newspaper, on a piece of work, or on emptiness. An eternity of dull hope hangs over them.

In the hall, carts roll by, with a faint, rubber-tired rumbling; radio music, from very far away, is etched against the azure silence of the window. I yawn, the hospital penetrates me and comforts me like an old nurse: there, there, it's nothing, it's all better, kiss the bump.

Just the same, I keep one eye on the door.

If only Nini would come. I want to see Nini, or anyone else, to keep in touch with the world I know: here, I am adrift in a strange world, I have lost the familiar clouds and branches, I almost miss the cold grayness of my old hideout ... everything is too illuminated, too precise: the shadows where I used to hide will dissolve, I will be recognized.... No, if in some extraordinary way a search warrant had reached this hospital, the verification would have had to be made right away, when I was still with the mother. And besides, I am Nini's sister, I bear her name, a name as anonymous as those which precede and follow it on the admissions registry. My name, here, is the name of my fracture ... an astragalus, did the doctor say? Not an anatomical chart in sight ... my face, it too is an astragalus, that's what they'll be looking at.

The floor nurse comes in, pushing a cart overflowing with boxes of bandages, plastic vials containing yellow, mauve, colorless liquids.... She makes a turn and aims her vehicle right at my corner.

"Which side for your injection?' she asks, seizing a hypodermic needle and a piece of cotton which she soaks in ether.

"Oh, it doesn't matter...."

"Lift up your nightgown and turn over."

I turn over and the gown, slit up the back, opens by itself onto the spectacle of my naked derrière. The "Get undressed" of these last years required a total disrobing and preluded a thorough search: even after several months of detention, with the weekly probe of the pants and bra, the supervisors would inspect me, after returning from Instructions, just as minutely: "Put your foot up on the stool. Cough ... All right." I had also obeyed quite thoroughly, from habit, the "Get undressed" of the nurse. Prison still surrounded me: I found it in my reflexes, the jumpiness, the stealth and the submissiveness of my reactions. You can't wash away overnight several years of clockwork routine and constant dissembling of self. When the body is turned loose, the mind, which up until then had been the only escape, becomes on the contrary the slave of mechanisms; the humility you used to fake turns into genuine embarrassment; me, one with all those loud mouths in there, I no longer dared, now, take the initiative in even the most natural of actions: at the mother's as well as at Pierre's, I always had on the tip of my tongue a "Please," a "May I," or I tended to act behind their backs; then I would remember that I was free, and become awkward and exaggerated.

I clung to that bewildered manner and, in an effort to overcome it, made terrible blunders, I was betrayed by old fears, and at the same time by a natural devil-may-care exuberance.... Furthermore, I didn't know much about the life Julien brought me into: at Central, I'd hung around more with criminals than actual tramps. Wanting to please Julien and do him honor by pleasing his friends, I hid my ignorance under a shrewd silence; or, struggling to appear worldly and cultivated, I would express myself like the heroines of the *Série Noire* or like an affected prude. But, invariably, I would be ridiculous.

Finally, at the hospital, I am starting off in the "first grade," like most of the patients in this room, undoubtedly: to break a bone can't become habitual like a chronic disease, for example, the astragalus, then, can also be a cover for my ineptitudes.

I think, my mind racing, since the nurse pulled the sheet back up over my rear, after injecting, very slowly, very painfully, the contents of a large syringe. I rub the place where the needle went in to make this new hurt circulate: it feels as though plates and pipelines of lead had been sunk into my hip and thigh. Little by little, the whirling in my head slows down, as a carnival wheel-of-chance comes to a stop, the images turn very slowly, hesitating before they settle, while the walls and ceiling drift off with a ponderous delicacy; the air around me solidifies and falls in big disembodied lumps onto the tiled floor, a black film seeps out of my eyelids.... Be careful, I must not close my eyes, or else I'll be done for. I don't want to go to sleep, I want to see as much as possible. I wonder, are they going to set my fracture under a general anesthetic, or am I already drugged enough? I can't feel anything anymore ... I'm going to ask. The neighbor on my left is an old woman, smiling, who woke up when the nurse came in and has been looking at me sympathetically ever since.

"Madame ..."

"Madame ..."

"Yes?"

"Excuse me for bothering you, but ..."

I started out in the tones of a "well-brought-up young lady," but something isn't working: it's not shyness that's cramping my throat like this; I can't hear myself speak, my tongue is enormous and inert, it chokes off the words, and the words themselves disintegrate as soon as they are put together; I try to remember what I wanted to say, but it all dissolves, I ...

"Shh," the lady says, "don't talk. Just rest, close your eyes. The anesthetic will work better if you are relaxed...."

So, they're going to put me to sleep some more. Good: sure that I'm not going to be in pain, I pull myself together, I fight. I latch onto an image, there, the picture on the cover of the match box, for instance. A province. *Aie,* I can't read anymore, let's see, let's guess: at Central, each group was named after a province, four groups, the matches in a box, the girls in a box, the ... no, I'm not asleep.

5

"... So I made my big goo-goo eyes at him, and I said, choking up a little: 'Doctor, it's unbearable, it's torturing me....' Net result, he had the frame taken away and a hoop put on. It's not quite as high, but you can still hide under it. Julien baby ..."

I feel witty, sparkling, if it were allowed I'd take my leg out of the cast, yes: by bending my foot up and pulling hard, like on a boot.

"What a sissy I've been these last two weeks, you can't imagine.... Oh, Julien, you're here...."

"Darling.... But how could I know it was so serious? Nini told me over the phone that you've been put into traction and that everything was fine! And then they operate on you, and I don't know a thing about it!..."

Julien is sitting next to my head, one elbow on the night table and one hand under the sheet on my hip.

"But Nini hasn't been here for three days, and ... it happened day before yesterday. You see, you came just in time for my resurrection. The first night, though, I finally had to ring for the nurse, I was yelling and I couldn't seem to stop....

So—for the neighbors' sake, you understand—I asked for something to quiet me down. I think they gave me some morphine. I banged around some more a little the next day, until this morning, really: I spent a horrible night, hugging my cast, with my knee pulled up under my chin.... And then, this morning, I saw an angel, the birds began to sing again, and ... here you are."

Julien looks at his watch:

"We still have a whole hour to talk. Tell me all about it. Tell me everything they did to you."

I laugh at the idea:

"It's not worth it! Anyhow, that would be hard, I slept through all the interesting parts. The rest of the time, there's just the routine of this joint: coffee and milk, meals at eleven and six (not much different from inside back there), the nurses, the penicillin. I can tell you, my behind hurts a lot more than my leg! Look."

I pull my gown halfway up my stomach: the penicillin shots they give me three times a day have left purple bruises on my hip, little crusted dots.... I think that when you're in a hospital you sort of enjoy showing off the ugliest thing you have: the person who has the most hideous scar, with the most stitches, the most enormous cast, the heaviest traction. And I, for Julien's benefit, instead of playing up my unblemished face and hands, exhibit skin riddled with holes and mottles, and am sorry I can't show him what's under my cast as well, and which, judging from the discoloration around my heel, must be even more compelling.

But Julien.... Today, his hand lies softly on me, without desire, it is visiting a sick person, it is a sister. I know what a woman is to him, a woman is a guitar, pleasant, but you have to remember to be gentle, it's been wounded but it would like to sing. Julien sweetly, skillfully, goes about making love, yet avoids getting too involved; it's back to the brotherly shadow, lonely little pet, and his kisses are light, as light as his hand, but no, I'm not that fragile!

"In a few hours I'll be sitting up. . . ."

I don't dare to yet: my foot is asleep, resting on a pillow supported on either side by bags of sand. This morning, I decided that I could wash by myself, I took the basin and told the nurse to go away; and, while she was washing the others, I scrubbed, rinsed, got off my skin the stale odors of chloroform, of cold sweat, the damp musty traces of pain.

Bit by bit, Nini lays in my supplies: she doesn't worry about cost, it's Julien who pays the bills, I have the most beautiful bathrobe, enough cigarettes for a month, enough makeup for a year, and even a pair of stretch slippers.

"When you start to walk," she says, sensibly, "you'll need something that supports your ankle."

". . . I'll make my exit in stretch slippers and a negligee with little flowers on it."

"Whoa there," Julien says, "it's only two days since your operation! In the meantime, I'll find you some dresses."

Julien "finds" things.

". . . Later, you'll have closets full, you'll change ten times a day if you feel like it. But for the moment, you'll have to get by with a few old rags: there's a time for everything."

Julien stands up and inspects the room: each bed is a little family council. During visiting hours the patients ignore one another, they isolate themselves in order to get back into their own lives: the visitors cluster around the beds, busy themselves tidying up the night tables, arranging the pillows, they furtively unwrap sweets or things they think are good for you: they know, the hospital doesn't know at all.

Nini comes two or three times a week, to replenish my provisions and take my orders; the rest of the time, I am an orphan. To avoid curious or pitying attentions from neighboring clans, I always read or sleep assiduously until it's time for the holy Thermometer. At exactly two o'clock, the nurse appears, thermometers in hand: "Visitors, please!" And, to speed the evacuation of the premises, she starts distributing the things, after having checked and vigorously shaken them down: "Temperatures!" The hospital reclaims its rights, the intruders flee. A few rebels linger in a prolonged embrace, a final touch to the flowers on the night table... They annoy me; if only they would leave, and these ladies come back to me, and again be bedridden creatures surrendered to solitude, to the imperatives of treatment, to the purring of the smoothly flowing hours.

"Is everything all right, with your neighbors? They're not too nosy?"

"It's a sure thing that after you leave your ears ought to be ringing.... The woman in the next bed, she's—as you can see—a mother, grandmother, aunt, mother-in-law ... her bedside is always jammed with relatives. She's here for a badly healed foot, she walked too soon and they had to put in a plate. But let's not talk about the patients...."

"And you, what do you tell them?"

"A whole lot of stuff: I was at my sister's, I was playing with the dog, he went down the terrace steps—I base my story on the layout of Pierre's place—to get down faster I jumped into the courtyard, a thing, my dear lady, which I used to do every day...."

I must have told it pretty well, yesterday the intern said: "That's what you get for playing with dogs!"

I go on:

"Besides Nini, you're my only visitor from the outside, but sometimes I have an intern or an attendant come and talk to me. For instance, there's a little male nurse ..."

Julien flinches imperceptibly, his pupils darken.

"... he promised to bring his camera. That would be nice, wouldn't it, some souvenir photos?"

"Are you completely nuts? Your picture is pasted in every police station, did you ever think of that? I swear, you really are a baby. I absolutely forbid you to have anything to do with that guy."

I don't object but I feel a little hurt: I would have liked it more if Julien could have confiscated the picture first. A picture of me!

"Oh, I'll ask him to give me the negatives, if you like."

"You know what you can get, for hiding a fugitive from the law?" Julien goes on in a low voice. "Nini and Pierre are a couple of jerks, O.K., but that doesn't mean they're not sticking their necks out because of you and you've got to remember that every second, with every word you say ..."

Oh how he bores me! I answer:

"Don't worry about my intelligence, I have plenty and some to spare ... instead, why not tell me just who you are."

"What?"

"Yes: my cousin, my brother-in-law, what should I tell them?"

Julien smiles, his eyes brighten again; he frames my face with his hands and holds it like that; our looks take root in each other, laughing with the same laugh, grow closer.... Oh

I love that kiss. Holy Thermometer, let my visitor stay here, next to me, under this hoop.

Julien draws away, rolls his eyes back, and murmurs in mocking accents.

"My fiancée …"

And so that's how I explain him to the ladies. Madame Plate and Madame Mirror compliment me and make wishes for our youth:

"You really make a charming couple…."

"If your children have curly hair like yours, and their father's eyes…. My Lord, what beautiful hair you have."

"Yes, marry him, do. He seems so nice, so honest!"

"Does he have a good job?"

I should say! A very distinguished position. That pays very well. To account for his irregular visits, I explain that my fiancé has to go on business trips. After that, I ask Madame Plate to lend me her knife, so that I can open the box of little cakes that Julien has left on the table.

Might as well shut them up with some butter creams.

6

After the newspaper and croissant sellers go through, we only see, until visiting hours, the members of the medical staff.

Every day, the Professor's assistant makes his rounds with the interns: but the Professor's assistant is someone we don't look at. For us, only God-the-Father exists, the one who baptized the instruments, the one who re-created us, with his own fingers or through intermediary fingers, God who charted the course of our operation, chose it from among various techniques. He has studied our x-rays to the very marrow, while our bodies reposed, inert, not knowing they were being observed: he judges, cuts, slices, grafts, but we are not allowed into his kitchen. Our meat is confiscated from us; and, if we should be permitted to use it again some day in the joy that lies ahead, Holy Efficiency, we shall never know by what means it got back to us.

God-the-Father passes through two or three times a week. On the days of the great man's visit, the cleaning girl moves the suitcases from under the beds, sweeps out the dead things

accumulated underneath and disinfects the bedpans with in-
habitual and ostentatious care; consequently, we get hit with
all her "tut tuts." No chance of getting the bedpan back before
the grand tour. We contract our sphincters, smooth the covers
of our beds, we animate our eyes and our lips. The love that we
all feel for Him inspires us into graceful poses, causes work or
reading matter that we feel most likely to catch his attention
to rise up out of our night tables: if he deigns to notice that,
surrounding bone, there is a woman, an uncarvable being who
works and thinks, if he puts down our x-rays for a minute to
look into our faces, if he gives us a smile or a word, then our
suffering and ignorance will fade away, then we will get well
and we will understand.

He approaches: feet and hands, nylon stockings and casts,
flush and pallor, everything melts and freezes into the same
humility. The head nurse whisks her cart in, makes sure no
cigarette is burning in the recesses of some night table, then
heads for the corner where the x-ray cabinet is kept.

It is a large white chest, with a heavy cover, mounted on
wheels; it contains our records. The head nurse hinges under
the cover and takes out our six case histories which she places
on the ends of our beds. She will make further notations on
them after the great man has left.

I, not even knowing what my blood type is, would love to
get my hands on that document. But how? The time that it's
out on the bed is too short, and the head nurse is glued to
the room, simultaneously surveying the hall down which the
cortege will come and whatever moves we might be trying to
make. The chest is not locked, but since none of us can walk....
Bribe one of the visitors? Get myself caught in flagrant auto-
curiosity, not on your life. I watch and wait: one day, the great

man will park himself before the bed opposite me, drawing away the general attention, and everyone will turn their backs on me long enough for me to fish up, leaf through, and replace it. I suspect, of course, that my electrocardiogram, the analyses of my various liquids and the photograph of my lungs will all be equally edifying: how could it be otherwise?

"... it hurts ..."

"I'm terribly tired (or weak, or constipated)."

"Look, Doctor, isn't that the beginning of a scab?"

No matter what startling or disturbing thing you may find you have, you must, upon referring it to Aesculapius, be prepared for this answer:

"Oh, come now, that's perfectly normal!"

So it's perfectly normal for me to feel my ankle turning and tossing in an abyss, that the small of my back should be arced like a rainbow, that pangs of hunger should be followed by pangs of nausea, that there should be a knot in my throat and my toes should lie on their plaster pedestal like five dead little blood sausages. Anyhow, none of this worries me: not only because "it's normal," but also because I welcome each fantasy, each of my body's reactions with resignation and with a certain possessiveness.

But what I would like to know is, how did they manage to reprieve my foot after having, at its first trial, guillotined it; what on earth could they have inserted in the way of a screw, plastic piece or plate to straighten it out again, and what this mysterious implement is, this apparatus that at times sends me across unsuspected thresholds of dizzying pain. At each shot of antibiotics, the pain of the immunization shots of childhood—the worst I had known till now—comes back multiplied by x; then I think of the benzine injections, of my conscious efforts to ruin my health, of what I used to say to Rolande: "If this doesn't work the way I want, I'll dislocate my foot, I'll give it a good whack with the stool.... "

My wish has been granted.

Sometimes, we ask God-the-Father questions:

"Sir ... or: Professor ..."

He never listens. Then one of his satellites leaves his wake and comes over to silence every question with a simple, mitigating sentence, invariably optimistic and vague:

"When will you be able to walk? Well ... very soon, very soon. Have a little more patience. What did they do to you? Oh, a magnificent job. A beautiful operation, don't you think?"

And the chorus of sub-satellites agrees in unison.

I begin to distrust their epithets: the more magnificent it is from their point of view, the more serious and drawn out from ours. We lack the clinical sense.

Then it seems to me that the Master stops at the foot of my bed for a long time. He gets out my x-rays, goes over to the window to study them in the daylight; I find myself separated from him by the sea of white jackets that crowds around his explanations, and he speaks so quickly, so softly, so hermetically, that my foot breaks up into incomprehensible bits and pieces and I grow desperate.... I get furious, I tell myself that he's showing off, that it's not possible for him to come straight from the operating table wearing such correct gloves and such white linen about his ankles. His words are dry, his remarks curt, his smile niggardly, to me he is a surgeon right out of the books.

However, he did speak to me once: I had been in traction for ten days, my heel pierced by a sort of knitting needle whose ends were attached to a horseshoe, from which a cord passed over a pulley and supported a fifteen-pound weight. I was encased up to the buttocks in an iron contraption; the upper part of my body was lowered as they'd raised the foot of the bed: a motionless cancan.... Me, who likes to sleep sprawled out on my stomach.... My neighbors comforted me: traction is a nuisance, of course, but it's nothing compared to an operation, you lucky thing, they put a pin in you, you won't have to have an operation, etc. I would have been glad to change places with them! I'd had enough of pulling on my cord and being torn apart. That morning, the Master noticed me:

"How old are you?" he asked me suddenly, tapping my most recent x-ray against the bed's crossbar.

He ignored my answer, however, and while they all got under way again, their steps following in his steps, I was left to blush and pale in peace.

"Very well, I'll have to see this girl's parents," he'd flung at the head nurse, who duly noted these instructions on my chart. At my sister's next visit, I bawled her out: if she'd only introduced herself as my mother, I suppose you don't think you look old enough, well what are we going to tell them now.... Nini unwrapped a bowl of strawberries and cream, and, while I was cooling off with them, went down to come to terms with the office. She came back, her cheeks flushed.

"It's all settled," she said. "I signed the permission, they'll go ahead as soon as they have the results of your tests."

"Go ahead?" I cried. "Go ahead with what?"

"Your ... well, your leg just isn't healing, there are some splinters, the head nurse didn't go into details, but ... they're going to operate on you fairly soon it seems."

All week, I held court in my bed: my cast making any thought of moving me quite impossible, the radiologist, the cardiologist, the hypodermic-givers from the lab all came to me. I made peepee where they wanted me to. I died of hunger several mornings running waiting for them, so afraid was I of lousing up my operation.

Finally, on the sixteenth day of having the pin in me, I absorbed the dawn Nembutal, and I waited to go to surgery, dozing. This time, I knew how to survive until I got to the table: you had to let your consciousness get fainter and fainter, and keep it dimmed like a night light from then on; avoid thinking, turn the colored pages of the book in slow motion, at their own speed; set your eyelids at "half-closed," provoke nothing, remember nothing. Around me, from a great distance, the humdrum of the morning went ahead, carts, masks, bedpans, smells: six brands of toilet water, an odor sullied, discolored by urine and medications.

The evening before, they had cut off my brace, they'd painted my leg yellow, they'd wrapped the thing up in an enormous foamy bandage; I'd put on an imperceptible touch of makeup, following the nurse's advice:

"Above all, don't put anything on your face, and remove that fingernail polish, will you?"

But even dead, I wanted to be attractive to God-the-Father.

At ten o'clock the attendants hoisted me onto the stretcher, the head nurse folded the covers back over me, slid two immaculate pillows under my head and my leg; and I left, waving greetings right and left with my finger tips, like a queen from her chariot.

In the room outside the operating room, where corridors haunted by silence had brought me, the head nurse leaned over me: I saw her face enlarged and I had time to see her eyes soften behind her glasses as her lips planted a good loud kiss on my cheek. She said: "See you later, little girl," and disappeared.

I was left alone, in that room full of clean shade. My records were resting on the foot of the stretcher, near my feet, which were placed together like those of the dead; but I was incapable of reaching for them, the foot of the stretcher was at the other end of the world, and after all, I didn't give a damn about those papers. I didn't give a damn about anything, I was dead, my arms were dead lying the length of my dead sides; only the wall was alive, it undulated and slowly spun around.

The intern on duty shattered my beatitude; he came in, inflicting an enormous noise and volume on the emptiness, spitting torrents of words and clouds of smoke. At the same time, I realized that he was speaking quietly and smoking his usual Gauloises; but my thinking and my senses no longer worked in the same dimensions.

"Well, baby," yelled the intern, "feeling O.K.? Don't feel like going to sleep?"

I thought "no, no," I tried to revive my expression.

And I died, my left hand held in the intern's glove, my right arm stiffened on the armrest, as soon as the anesthetist began to push down the plunger of the large syringe of pentothal. I died with an agreeable tingling in my temples, without having witnessed the entrance of God.

I went up to the operating room three times in this fashion: when the space left by the removal of my astragalus didn't fill in, they broke through the gap with two new pins, one in my heel and one in my ankle; the four stirrups emerging from the plaster, and attached with adhesive tape. On one of the head nurse's days off, I finally succeeded in sneaking the records, left out since breakfast by her replacement, and in copying down the accounts of the operations. I learned some new words: resection, abrasion, astragalectomy, arthrodesis....

Julien comes to see me, irregularly; as summer ripens, he brings fruit and bottles of wine, he goes out during the visit to buy ice cream for me and my neighbors. Propped up on my pillows, I watch him cross the room, the blond smile, the polite and ridiculous look with his five or six vanilla-strawberry cones balanced in his fingers. The whole room, except for me, is engaged to him. We seem naive and carefree, we hold hands.

"Ah! Anne, I wish you would come back.... The night you went into the hospital, I slept at Pierre's, in your bed. When I came into the room, I saw you, I breathed you, you were still there.... "

I lean against him, I stain the shoulder of his shirt with my face powder; his jacket is thrown over the end of the bed, the layers are peeled away one by one, we find each other again.... Every word is immense with hope and emptiness, there is no room for us on earth: either running away or jail, always, and always alone.

"I wish you would come back...."

"But I don't want to go back there!"

"You must, all the same.... Until they can take your cast off, don't forget that you're Nini's sister.... Afterward, I'll get something else, in Paris probably. Try to find out approximately when you'll be discharged."

"By the way, Julien, did you find out what 'arthrodesis' means?"

During his last visit, I'd given him the copies of my records with the mission of decoding them.

"Yes; it means 'locked.' You won't be able to bend your foot."

"You might lose it," "I'll have to see this girl's parents," and now "locked."... My mascara comes off on the white shoulder, the more I cry the more it stings, the more it stings the more I cry, ah, damned mascara. I'll never stand on my tiptoes again, good-bye high heels, I'll limp and you'll be a crutch for a crippled girl, who perhaps won't ever know what you wanted from her, who won't even know how to find herself.... The future reels: now how can I be flip, insolent? How do I dare even show my face? Rolande ...

I think, I withdraw, I lie with my head on Julien's arm until the end of the visit, silent, mechanical, sniffling back my tears. He rocks me, caresses me with little stories and sweetly says he doesn't give a damn about my problem. Surgeons, there are plenty of others, later we'll take you to the superspecialists and.... But of course, stupid, you'll be running around again as good as new.

The next day, I ask the intern if I can leave.

The guy examines my x-rays, pulls down the sheet, bends my knee, straightens my toes, cool and unswollen at present, but still inert: with his shirt unbuttoned on a triangle of hair, his hips wrapped in a white apron which flaps against his legs, he resembles a large animal dressed up as a butcher. He looks at me, then notices the bottle of Monbazillac on the little table and smiles:

"You don't like it here with us? Does your mama allow you to drink like that?" Then:

"I think that you can leave: ask the Doctor, but I don't see why not.... You'll have to come back and see us to have your cast removed."

"But ... can't I leave ... right away?"

"That ... I don't know."

Julien will be coming back in a while, he's got to take me away.... I catch the head nurse: she always makes sure that every permission is scrupulously signed and approved by the chief doctors on duty, but in front of us she rather likes to play the big shot. At eleven, as she hands me my plate, she gives me the go-ahead:

"I've put through your dismissal slip, you're leaving this afternoon. Do you want an ambulance, or is someone coming to get you?"

"No, no, I've someone coming."

The ward girl takes our plates, carries them to the central table, empties the leftovers in the can. She wipes the blue Formica table top with a cloth, blue like the walls and June, there, in the window. A torpid stifling heat comes in, in waves; the window glistens, as though the paint were sweating. I am leaving, I am getting out of this pleasant stupor, out of my bed in the sun, I am leaving the hospital.

A cop came, yesterday: he was looking for "a minor who was injured on the highway." He came straight to my bed, my voice faltered and my back was drenched with sweat; but I was still going on about the dog and terrace when he turned out his heel. I later learned that the minor in question was in the room next door; a motor-scooter accident, a broken knee. Even so, what a scare! Julien is right: the little sister, a prey to accidental or well-meant questions, would be less of a menace if she were around.

It seems to me that I can hear Pierre: "Think of it, a mere kid, if she gets us all sent up...." O.K., O.K., I'm coming back. But this time I'm not going to be a fool: I've got a pedigree, an astragalectomy, and Julien, Julien who you suck around because he's got dough.... Julien is here, he'll make you swallow your filthy words, and soon I'll be walking all over you, I also.

"You're taking me with you?"

Where, that's understood: all those words, prison, break,

police, I've learned to swallow. Whenever I used them, even in a whisper, during Julien's first visits, they always seemed to boom out in a sudden silence; and the whole room, patients and visitors, would turn toward me, alerted and indignant. In a second my word created a cataclysm, I was recognized, dragged out, lynched.... Then, I would notice that there was nothing wrong, that no one had heard a thing or moved a muscle. Yes, Julien would have; his face would rebuke me, by an imperceptible flicker in its expression, a shadow, an annoyed look; lord, another blunder, Anne.... What can I do, to please Julien? How reconcile what I know about him with what I see? I put a foot—a stiffened foot—into the life of a hoodlum and everything about it surprises me, everything intrigues me.... Julien, a burglar? At any rate, it's thanks to the loot he picks up at night over perilous garden walls that my leg has been healed. Surgery, if you're not insured, is thirty or forty bucks a day, and then there was my board at Pierre's, all kinds of expenses.... Julien is making me a golden leg. Just the same, I refuse to be sanctimoniously grateful: I'm sure that I myself would have been able, I would have even been obliged to do the same, if I had spotted in my headlights, one freezing spring night, a man who needed me in order to complete his liberation.

"You know, if you'd been an old bag, I would have done the same thing...."

I'm sure, sweetheart. And it would have been much easier, I know. If by some misfortune I love you, or if, even worse, you start loving me, you'll always ruin it, you'll refuse to accept it, for imaginary and wrong reasons.... They're wrong, they're wrong.... So let's just blame it on our youth, let's be very tender brothers, let's bury all our memories, since that's what you want. Julien is trembling:

"Oh! If it weren't for your cast ..."

You'll take me away: that's no longer an issue.

... Here we are back at Pierre's again, in our room. I am sitting on the floor and Julien on the edge of the bed; we're not touching each other; only, the absentminded comb of his fingers lifts my hair off the back of my neck. It's very hot. Lazily, we run sentences together, we talk about cool and restful things, about books, our travels around our cells; then, about cold things, about deserted roads, vain pilgrimages.... I, I am dead and disowned, I welcome everything starting from that death, under the black trees, and the rest ... the rest is buried with what they used to know about me, what they're searching for: what sort of life could photographs and fingerprints have? That's all that's left of the past, but ... hell! It's still very much there all the same. And now this foot, on top of everything ...

"Look, with my crutches, I'll be able to get in anywhere. Later, we could make a fake cast, removable.... "

"To make it look even more realistic, we could cut your leg out entirely and hold your stockings up with thumbtacks. But, kidding aside, you could almost wear a stocking right now, over that cast!"

Modestly, I contemplate my footgear: it's true that it is pretty, a still immaculate pastel pink, the pins held in place by fresh adhesive tape....

"It's better than it was, I must admit...."

The tobacco dries our mouths; we smoke anyhow, automatically. Nini has begrudged us an ashtray, a glass saucer from the bar, shallow, inadequate. It's already overflowing. "Wait, don't get ashes all over the floor, she'll just get pissed off again tomorrow. Here's something better."

And Julien pulls the bidet, by its iron legs, out from under the sink. We flick our cigarettes into it: We are saved, we have all the time in the world; hot stagnating time, time which passes minute by minute, quietly, calmly, whispering.

7

Since this leg began making its minor repairs in the dark, it must have gotten a thousand times tougher than the other leg, which never had these little problems. I requisition knitting needles for it from Nini, I have a quart of eau de cologne a week bought for it and I swipe knife blades from the kitchen. It itches, inside there: I scratch with my blade, then I dribble cyprus or lavender down along the tibia and the calf. Pierre sniffs with contempt: "Still pouring perfume all over yourself!"

I rush through meals, and flee on my crutches to the front or back of the house. Once Pierre is off pushing his deals and Nini to her housework, I take off my bathrobe and tan myself, naked, my eyes closed under the torrid sky. Streams of sweat run together over my skin and drip into the grass, my cast tightens, melts. I hobble into the laundry, plunge myself into the tub, my leg propped on the edge out of the water: this is important, more than ever I have to live with my legs spread apart, the pins pierce through the bones and one drop of water could cause an infection. Cleaning my toes, too, requires a great deal of care: the mere touch of the washcloth irritates them. One morning I took the adhesive tape off the pins, and, layer by layer, cut a circle in the plaster around one of them, to see. I saw a metal stem plunging into dark red, tight, swollen flesh; by pushing and pulling, I got one of the pins to move; but the other one is still wedged tight. I think about what I'll have to go through when they pull it out, I think about that hideous round patch of leg and I feel like crying. I've had enough, I'd like to have it over with.

And, whether because they'd be pleased to see me getting around, or clear me out of the place, everyone else would dearly like to have it over with too: actually, Pierre would be delighted if I did something stupid. Why do I have to wait for Julien? What more do I need from him?

"Sure, of course, you have to stay near the hospital. But what about later on? What are you planning to do?"

Pierre pensively pulls on his accordion and picks out mechanical exercises, one eye on his fingering, one eye on me, a chord, a phrase. He takes off his undershirt and settles the greasy rolls of fat over the belt of his shorts. I am sitting across from him in pants and a bra, the heat makes it seem all right.

"What? ... But Pierre, I'll be walking, I'll make out all right."

"Make out all right. But you're not walking, at present. Let's suppose. ... Julien must have told you, you must be aware that, *for you*, he's taking risks. The dough ..."

"Don't worry, we're keeping track of that, that will all be settled between him and me."

But what is he driving at?

"Ah! Between him and you! And *sometime*, but what about now?"

Pierre strums furiously, up and down the scales with fingers strangely mismatched to the rest of his body: agile, graceful, precise fingers attached to a bellowing, shaking mass of jelly.

"Do you realize that he hasn't been around for ten days?"

"He's working!... And besides, with his restriction, it doesn't pay for him to be seen around here too much."

"Oh sure! You know all the angles! And what if he doesn't come back, what if he gets caught? Did you ever think of that?"

Oh yes, Pierre, I've thought of that. I think about it every hour, every second. The thought of Julien wakes me up and keeps me awake all night listening to every car, every door, every footstep. Perhaps in this way I can keep tragedy and darkness from his path ... be careful, Julien. As for me, now, I can walk: on one or two or three legs, I will always be able to walk far enough to find you, to rescue you in my turn, if need be. But please be careful.... I study the tip of my cigarette:

"Julien always comes back in the end," I say.

"Yes, the last time we expected him for dinner he showed up two years later."

"Well, if it comes to that, we'll help him. *I'll* help him. Alter settling accounts with you, of course. But, since Julien always pays you several weeks in advance, I don't think there's any point in moving me out quite yet. What can you expect, I'm pooped."

(Oh! All this talk about accounts!)

"You wouldn't have to move out anyway," Pierre says. "The day you can walk out the door, O.K. But wouldn't you like to go out and hustle like I go off to the factory? And at night have clients follow you home, real big spenders ... "

"... and pimps."

I add that because Pierre is appraising my figure with studied indifference and I know perfectly well what he's leading up to. When the place was an inn, I doubt very much that the four rooms, upstairs, were simple tourist accommodations.

I imagine Nini changing the moth-eaten towels and looking for little condoms in her money pocket, thank you sir. At the bar on payday night—a large glass of soda water for me—Pierre would make short work of building up a clientele for me.

He turns a page of his exercise book and says:

"You see, since we serve food here, nobody gets in unless he has a clean record: if someone came to see you, it would be because he had my permission. It's already bad enough that we had to give this address at the hospital.... I hope you haven't arranged to have any mail sent here?"

"I already told you I don't want to get involved with anyone!"

"Involved, no, but.... I don't know: the other patients, the nurses ..."

I feel like striking back at him:

"Oh, the address was clearly written on my temperature chart, at the foot of the bed. If someone took it down, I really can't help it. At any rate, it's Nini who gets the mail, all she has to do is send it back."

I can hardly keep from bursting out laughing. If they only knew what I thought of their respectable whorehouse!

On Sundays, Pierre and Nini leave for the whole day, taking the kid with them and leaving me the mother: they bought a cottage for their old age, and are hurrying to paint and furnish it, and put a fence around it, in order to sell the roadhouse and retire to the country for good.

On Saturday, Nini fixes something to eat for her mother-in-law and me, that is, she boils some eggs and potatoes, leaving it up to me to peel them, and "there are some canned things in the cupboard, if you get hungry." She takes the keys to the house and on Sunday morning, just as I'm giving up my vigil, Julien won't be coming—and am about to go to sleep in the first rays of sunshine, she pokes her head in my door and cries:

"We're off. If someone knocks or telephones, be sure not to answer. See you this evening."

I answer that I won't answer and I go to sleep, until it's time for the mother-in-law's morning coffee. That one, when she's not eating or sleeping!... She spends her days sitting in the kitchen, hands flat in front of her on the marble table, the greenish hands of a corpse; she doesn't move or say a word, and only rouses herself at the smell of food, which she devours like a ravenous beast, voraciously, filthily. There is something hallucinating about these Sunday tête-à-têtes.

The only door that Nini can't padlock is the door of the giant refrigerator, a restaurant model you could hang whole sides of beef in, which serves at present for storing bottles. Behind the mother-in-law's back I mix up atrocious drinks inside it. The thing that gives me the most trouble is lugging my glass around: I can't use my hands because I need them for my crutches. So I move the glass a foot at a time, across the floor, between steps; when I get to the terrace I lie down, wearing only my cast, and fill myself with alcohol and sunshine.

By the time the owners get back, I've taken a bath in the laundry, rinsed out my mouth, and am clean down to my knee, clearheaded and dying of thirst:

"That sun, it really dries you out."

Poor Pierre, who wants me to work at home, and whose stolen whiskey is undoubtedly reserved for just that sort of entertainment.

I resume the conversation:

"I'm perfectly willing, but I wonder if Julien would like to find out that he's a pimp."

"Oh, pimp, pimp, that's just a word. He'd be very pleased on the contrary: he doesn't like being in debt. Anyhow, you're not married to him, are you?"

And Pierre points out to me that the money would not be considered as what I've earned, but as what I owe; that he would only accept it under those conditions, in any case; that I would surely be able to find a way, later, to explain the whole thing to the person I call, seriously! "my man," and that if I do it in the right way, he wouldn't be offended:

"Women are always so good at that sort of line...."

Pierre being clearly within his rights, Julien in the dark, and myself a mere intermediary, the arrangement should satisfy every moral demand.

To hell with morality, I'm going to warn Julien.

I even throw in my own two cents:

"Just *one* of Pierre's vulgar remarks should buy me a month's free room and board, you know...."

Julien had arrived in the middle of the night, like the last time: Nini, furious at having to jump out of bed to open the gate for him, had said, when she brought up our breakfast tray at around eleven:

"You got me once, but from now on you can just keep ringing.... You're too much, I must say! At two A.M., without having telephoned or written, what do you do, you turn up like you're doing me some sort of a favor. I'm going to go back to the way things were when the hotel was open: at eleven o'clock I'm going to lock everything up and let the dog out."

This night, Julien had jumped over the wall, patted the mutt and gotten in through a ground floor window: from there on in the doors are open, and mine isn't even locked every night. Evenings when I go up to bed with my nerves on edge and a regret at having changed prisons, I double-lock myself into my room; it consoles and liberates me to bolt the door of my jail myself. On the other hand, on evenings when the dinner was good, when our stomachs digesting the same food together and the mingled sounds—Nini's dishwashing, Pierre's accordion—cast a pleasant sleepiness over the night, I simply gave the door a push: if they went to the bathroom during the night, perhaps they'd notice, in passing, the open door, the carelessness, the lack of modesty.... One morning Nini reminded me that in leaving my door half-open like that I'd warp the wood, and who's going to pay the carpenter, me?

So, even on friendly evenings I leave the door on the latch.

Julien opened it so quietly that I wouldn't have waked up, if I had been asleep. But I wasn't sleeping. I never sleep. At least, I have the impression of being too alive, when Julien comes, and no sooner gets into bed than is gone again: I would like to be as tired as he and sleep beside him, instead of interfering with his sleep, plaguing him and bothering him:

"Kitten," he says, "forgive me, I'm dead.... "

I sulk off to the other edge of the bed, I pretend to be asleep, while waiting to be.... Do I really want this man so much? He eases my idleness and pain, he is my joy, yes, but.... If I were able to hope for something else, some other form of pleasure, would I have chosen him?

Tonight, Julien is wide awake:

"What a fit she'll have, tomorrow morning! Too bad, I'm going down to the kitchen, I'm thirsty. Do you want me to bring you something to drink?"

"Yes, bring me a glass of water. With five times that amount of Ricard."

The hours go by. Naked, without moving, drowned in warmth, we breathe the heavy air that flows in through the shutters.

"Are there some shirts of mine here?" Julien suddenly asks.

"Yes, I washed and ironed the whole bag for you, this week. Nini told me that, since I called myself your wife, it was up to me to take care of your laundry."

"No, really? She made you work, with your leg?"

"I don't wash with my legs. It's O.K., it's fun to me. I hang them out of the window, over there, she gets miffed, the neighbors are going to ask who's living in the room, it looks like a slum, etc. Imagine, of course the next day I'm at it again. I'm climbing up on the sink and loosening it from the wall for good, I'm spotting their sheets, in short, I'm trying to make their lives impossible.... Maybe so, maybe so, Julien, all the same I'd give my eye teeth to get out of here...."

Julien explains that he came early because a new problem had come up, a guy on the lam who had landed at his mother's asking to be hidden: he was going to try and get him put up here. The shirts, they were to be for him.

"But they've already raised such a stink, about me...."

"Huh! If you knew the number of guys I've brought them already! They holler, but the love of money is stronger, they always end up agreeing."

"And what do you bring them in the line of women?"

"Ah! They've told you that too. I don't know, I don't remember. Anne, in any case, you're the only one for me. Just believe that, please: it's you, Anne, you...."

I drop my questions. I'm lying here, in those other women's

place, and this moment belongs to me, to me alone. Whether they begged, shouted, ordered, the favors, the kindnesses and the duties rendered have gone with them, and it's me, me.... Tomorrow... what does tomorrow matter? Tomorrow hasn't begun yet.

"... So," Julien continues, "if they agree, I'll give my place a call and the guy can get himself over here for the introductions."

"That means you'll stay here, oh, great!"

Tomorrow can begin now: I know what it will be like. Julien will have his worried look, he'll stay close to the phone, and with his thoughts centered on something else I'll be able to circle around him on my crutches without disturbing him. I'll be the guitar, he'll touch me with an abstracted gentleness and put me aside again. What could really keep Julien from thinking about what he wants, what he wants when he's burdened with so many duties and responsibilities?

Pierre sniggers:

"Saint Julien, back again today?"

So Julien talks about moral satisfaction, Pierre makes puns (it's true that he makes quite good ones), you're right but I'm not wrong: they're not trying to convince each other, they're just expressing themselves, for hours on end. And we, the women, listen in silence, Nini over her ovens, me behind my cigarette.

This lunch is going to be some fun! And this guy, this ...

"What does this buddy of yours call himself?"

"He calls himself Pedro, which goes with his personality. But, for the moment, you'll address him as 'Father,' like everyone else.

"Yes: from the results of the studies made with his asshole, his anal mysticism, and his natural vice, the best thing he could come up with was to dress as a priest."

At night, we dine with a seminarian in a too-new habit. Upon arriving, Pedro had said to me:

"Ah, it's you, Anne! Delighted.... Julien has talked so much about you and your ... accident. How is your leg?"

"How do you do, Father. It's better, thank you."

I had answered coldly: I don't want to establish a complicity of fugitives between myself and this Pedro of the velvet eyes, who speaks too politely and looks like a shiny chestnut. From what one can discern under the folds of the ecclesiastic vestment, he seems to be perfectly built and muscled, with that effeminacy, that Latin languor, appearing in his accent and gestures: Pedro claims to be a truant from the Midi, so he comes on with self-assured openness, effusive words halted abruptly by silences: but the break is too clean, he lacks the long-windedness, the rephrasing of spontaneous speech. Pedro works at offering glimpses of himself, but I don't suppose here's really very much to be discovered: he's a good-looking guy, a good talker, a slick job. Defrocked and dressed like everyone else, he must nevertheless attract attention, by his exaggerated naturalness. Even the hairs of his mustache seem to have been planted.

He's to sleep in the room next to mine. We go upstairs chatting in a bunch; on the landing, we say good night to each other. But as the conversation doesn't seem to be ending and I have nothing to add to it but monosyllables and forced smiles, I make it into my room and start washing.

For Julien's sake, it's important that I look attractive to Pedro, that I make myself beautiful, that I overwhelm by my wit and wisdom.... I want to erase what he knows and sees, the crutches, the helplessness, the awkwardness, the minor ... even though he can't be so old himself: twenty-four, maybe twenty-five? A mere kid. After all, the only advantage he has over me is that he can walk, a small detail that doesn't keep him from letting Julien help him out, come on now, forget it!

I tuck myself into bed: in a while Julien will find his place warm and waiting, and I'll slide over onto the cool part of the sheet. I arrange my hands on a book, I pull down the top of my old nightgown a little.

Pedro walks in with Julien, excusing himself profusely:

"Just a couple words more, Anne, and I'll leave you alone...."

They confer in front of the closet mirror, hastily, without forming their words. I imagine them in prison garb, speaking this way during the daily walk. It doesn't occur to them to sit down, they pace back and forth as they talk, go ahead, parade right around the bed while you're at it! I turn the pages of my book, absorbed, I feel like throwing it in their faces: good Lord, won't they ever stop?

This gallant priest, this half-assed jerk!

All the same, the next morning, we sit around together after coffee, Pedro and I. We've decided to forget about our educations and our good families; but, to impress each other, other grounds for vanity being taboo or still unclear, these are nevertheless the first subjects we inflict on each other.

Imitations, quotes, suspenseful pauses. Pedro has left his habit hanging up: he's wearing shorts and an undershirt, with tennis shoes: this morning, before coffee, he put himself through a series of setting-up exercises, the kid must be in shape, a puffing and panting routine followed by immersions and ablutions in the laundry tub.

Gone, my lovely hours dressed like Eve! An Adam perfumed with aftershave lotion is chasing me from the only paradise I had: the laundry.

Pedro stands up and stretches, endlessly:

"All right," he says. "This afternoon, I'm going to go into town: to see a few friends. Is there anything you need, Anne?"

His hands flat on his pectoral muscles, planted on the perfect columns of his legs, he reeks of health.

"No, thanks.... Oh, yes, could you bring back the papers?"

Thus Pedro becomes my purveyor of reading matter. He reads a lot himself, books appropriate to his role in life: *The Thief's Journal*, locksmith manuals; and, for the subway, Dr. Locard's *Treatise on Criminology* or the *Palace Gazette*.

For, weary of innocent or intentional "Hello, Father," of seats given up respectfully on public transports, and of the clamminess of long skirts, Pedro has changed back into civilian summer attire.

He got back several nights in a row at dawn: it must have paid off, for now he changes his duds every morning. Immaculate shirt, pearl-gray set of threads, and various hats: despite the books and the briefcase, he still looks like anything but a college man. His studies don't come across at all; and his secrets are obvious, obvious.... When he's not there, and even when he is, Pierre kids him unmercifully:

"Those shirts, on nights when there's a full moon, they still get by, but this winter you'll be piercing the fog with them: Light your way with your shirt, and you leave your hands free!"

Sometimes, Julien calls him up and they meet at mysterious places. They get back together, at dawn: I welcome home a man whose eyes are brilliant with fatigue, whose face is covered with dried sweat, with dust, and with a growth of beard.

On these occasions Pedro dispenses with his exercises and sleeps until dinnertime. And we, we talk with the lucidity of that second wind born of exhaustion: for I sleep even less, these nights.

As for Pierre, he cools the irony and goes through the loot. However, he could be nasty without breaking me up too much: Pedro has stayed out all night instead of sleeping with his wife.

I stumbled on this quite by chance; and it bothers me a little, like when in Central I would cheerfully open up the lock of a cell—pardon me, of a room—and catch two girls inside who'd had themselves locked in by a third one. Luckily, here, Pedro and Nini don't know that I know: that doesn't make me any the less bothered, but it lets them act friendly or indifferent to me honestly, instead of having to take me in and butter me up.

On that particular afternoon, it was too hot to take a sunbath before three or four o'clock; Pedro, Nini and I had dawdled, at lunch, over cold, raw, bright-colored things, not drinking and with only one pressing idea on our minds: to take a nap in the shade from the shutters, upstairs. What a wonderful sleep I'd had, stretched out on the big bed, a wet cloth over my toes, my cast saturated with eau de cologne! At two, I'd felt like taking a bath in the laundry, and I'd gone back downstairs on my crutches.

From practicing with my two sticks of wood, I've made them into two real legs, light and quiet; on my crutches I dance, I whirl around, I swing, like those puppets attached between two wooden sticks that you tighten more or less to make the acrobat somersault on his wire. I put down my three feet, one, two-three, one, two-three, with skill and synchronism; I go downstairs at top speed, I raise the crutches to maneuver the turn on the landing on my heel, and I come out into the ballroom. A half-partition separates this room from the bar, and, in the angle of this partition there is a sofa, a resting place that guests flop down on, a haven for people who don't have a room; on it you can take a nap or have a chat, the laundry gets piled up there: this sofa is a whole separate room unto itself.

So I came in, my crutches soundless on the resonant floor. When I got to the sofa, Nini was sound asleep on it, turned toward the wall, the spread pulled up over her ears; and Pedro was sneaking off among the telephone books stacked behind the bar, whistling softly, displaying a naked and flawless back.

He gave the bar gate a shove and came toward me, his shorts and arms all dusty:

"I give up. I'll look up the number at the telephone company. It's really too filthy here."

"Oh you know," I said frankly, "it's always filthy backstage.... And that's where we live, you and I especially, wouldn't you say?"

Pedro picked up his undershirt which had been thrown over the sewing machine, two feet from the bottom of the bed; and, without glancing at Nini who still lay wrapped in innocence, he went out onto the terrace. I made off for the laundry faucet and its avalanche of pure little beads: what fortitude, those two, in all this heat!

I wasn't the first to mention it, nor was Julien: we brought it up at the same moment, and instantly collapsed into the same fit of laughter. Finally, Julien said:

"Well, get him! I hide him out, I shell out the down payment, I show him the ropes.... And he, instead of pulling out when he's on his feet again, he settles in! And starts making out!"

"But honey, he's unemployed.... He can't work all by himself, you have to take him by the hand: his nightly escapades, I'm sure they're just a lot of shit like everything else."

"'You want to make the haul? Well then, start climbing!' Imagine, I have to push him up and pull him down. If you ever saw a guy in a bind.... But a ground floor job, now that's another story, he's fearless, a real lion."

Julien tells me that Pedro gave him fifty thousand francs from one of their last jobs "to contribute to my hospital expenses"; that furthermore, he intends to discreetly do away with me when I leave here, in order to assure the safety of his hosts by my definitive silence, or, more exactly, the security of his pad.

"A sack, meals, and sex: well worth the price of a brat like me, naturally. But it doesn't make sense: why take the trouble to bail me out when I've already ceased to exist."

...Next, he suggested to Julien, very grandly, that they share Nini:

"So that I have no reason to envy him, no doubt," says Julien. "For a change, one of these days he's going to start coming on with you: you'll see, he'll get around to that, too. Unemployed, you say? Well hardly, he doesn't even have time to keep score on his tricks, he dreams about them at night. But watch out, Anne: watch out for Pedro, be can be very, very dangerous."

"Just let him try his keys in this door! Yes, those uncut keys he files away at for days on end at Pierre's workbench. Let him try them on Nini, on anybody else, but he'd better not have the nerve to try them on me."

He soon does have the nerve, however.

He prowls around, like a big, well-fed, unerring wolf; patiently, he plants little obstacles in his trail, which he deems likely to intrigue or excite me: intimate garments which he leaves here and there, shirts which he asks me, "Oh, just a little around the neck and cuffs," to be good enough to wash for him.

I wring out his nylon, I inhale his toilet water, I accept his gallantries: I don't have that much else to do.

He speaks of "Woman" with the devotion of an Oriental troubadour:

"But Anne, she's not a woman, she's a little man! Right, Anne? A little man very cleverly disguised.... You must have very pretty breasts. No?"

A "friendly" discussion: Pedro's gaze down the front of my dress is completely fraternal, respectfully charmed. Impassive, Nini clears the table. Her sharp, quick movements rebuke our inertia, the digestive laziness that slumps us in our chairs, leaning way back, stomachs proffered, legs stretched out and lifeless. As the plates and leftovers disappear, the ashtray resting between Pedro and me seems to grow in size: on the marble of the table it stands out like a sin. Nini has finished clearing: with a wet rag in her hand she goes after the crumbs and rings, wiping the table in wide soapy circles. She leans over a little further, rubs our places, picks up the ashtray which she goes and empties in the garbage; she puts it back, cleaned, irreproachably equidistant from Pedro and me. Just watch us sit there, cluttering it up with butts and cluttering up the kitchen all afternoon. Nevertheless, good hostess, good listener, she remains silent, smiles at Pedro's jokes, keeps busy and mechanical.

I suddenly wonder if, when the roadhouse was open, she didn't used to make a little on the side from tips—waiting on table, of course.

She says, without looking at me:

"At twenty, it's normal to have pretty breasts. Especially if you haven't had any kids."

Nini hasn't had kids, but I don't think she ever had breasts even so. How can Pedro apply himself to this girl's arid chest without repulsion?

"If you like," I say disdainfully, "I'll take off my bra, and I then you can get a better idea."

To change the subject, Pedro asks Nini to bring a bottle of champagne.

"Are you out of your head? What do you want champagne for?"

"To drink," Pedro explains. "We've talked a lot, which makes you thirsty. What do you think, Anne?"

When it comes to drinking, I'm always for it. Nini agrees to open the refrigerator: she'll put this on Pedro's bill, and after all, the customer is king. If it pleases the lady and gentleman to get stewed at this hour and in this heat.... With severity, she puts the bottle and two glasses on the table, then goes back to her dishes.

"Oh, oh Nini!" says Pedro.

That fake southern "oh, oh" that irritates me and unnerves me, that baying he punctuates his remarks with ... "Oh! Ah! Hey! Huh!"

"Is Nini angry? Come on, give us a little smile. Get a glass and come have a taste."

"Me, drink? ... You know perfectly well that I don't drink. I'm not allowed to: my heart ..."

The diffuse network of blood vessels in her cheekbones, then, which I thought were the dregs of too much wine, are from her heart. Pedro, you're not going to go and hurt Nini's little heart, now are you? Let's just the two of us drink: my heart can go pitter-pat in safety.

"Anne, Anne, you use your head too much."

"Well, I can't exactly use my legs!"

Pedro patiently works at the cork, which begins to loosen slowly; pop, it flies off behind the glass cupboard; and the gold liquid, promptly channeled into a glass with a twist of the wrist, gushes out making little noises. It's this ritual that I love, more than the pale taste and the bubbles in my nose. Glassful by glassful, we empty the bottle; Nini, disgusted, has vanished upstairs.

As the wine warms my body, my head cools off, and Pedro's head moves away, begins to float; soon none of Pedro has any consistency, any importance; he can go on talking and moving, he doesn't bother me, but not in the slightest.

I have drawn a circle, I am alone inside it, perfectly centered, outside impressions strike and grow confused, I let them get away and lose themselves, I couldn't care less. I hear, I understand, I answer; my speech is a little garbled, perhaps, but my thinking concentrates itself, clears; everything revolves around one phrase, unique, fixed, a phrase I look at, a signpost, a stairway:

"But watch out, Anne...."

Yes, Julien, don't worry: the little joke is over.

"Would you hand me my legs, Pedro? I am completely incapable of hopping over to the wall. I've tied one on at your expense, next time it'll be on me.... For the moment, I think the best thing to do is to go and recover from this one in bed."

"Come, Anne, I'll carry you...."

"And you'll carry me into your room.... No thank you. Hand me my transportation, I'm perfectly able to get to my *own* bed."

At that sofa resting-place I come to a halt ... and there I stay. Through hall-closed lids, in a gilded fog, I see Pedro going back and forth in front of the bed. But, out of deference to Nini perhaps, he makes no attempt to stop there.

8

Julien is taking me away today.

In the emptied room, grown larger, we keep looking for things in places where we used to find them with our eyes closed or the lights out; then, we remember:

"Oh, heck, I packed all my toilet articles in the bottom of the bag. Lend me your comb."

Nini won't find one butt, one speck of ash: the ashtray has been washed, and I've dusted underneath the bed with my crutch with a rag wrapped around it, which I've stashed in the bottom of the wastebasket.

We feel like we're getting out of jail. Julien inspects the closet one last time, gives the bags a kick:

"I'll take these down, and at the same time get hold of Pierre so that he can give me back my stuff, tools, laundry.... He'd better not hold his breath till I set foot back here again...."

"Don't take Pedro's files," I say.

"Oh him, he can drop dead. If you'd been just a little more of a dumbbell, I might have walked in on a real gangbang. Come on, baby, let's get moving."

At tea time, we're still there, sitting around the marble table. Pierre is being polite, a few cuts above normal: since giving Julien back his things, he realizes that the birds are leaving the nest for good.

"Nini, when the kid has to have her cast taken off, I'm going to come by and pick you up, it would look better if her sister went with her. Just take you a couple of hours."

"You're right, you're right, Julien," says Nini, overenthusiastically. "You could even come the night before and sleep here, so as to be on the spot, don't you think, Pierre? You'll always be welcome...."

"It's a thought, we'll see": Julien puts her off gently. But he's not forgotten the state he found me in yesterday afternoon; I was double-locked into my room, curled up around my rage in the armchair, amusing myself by figuring out the details of an insane plan of escape. One look, and he was off again to make the final arrangements at my new drop. I am expected, I don't know yet by whom, but I know where: in Paris.

I'm coming back, Paris, well ahead of time. No need to have cried, you were right, Cine.

In the taxi, Julien informs me that my hostess is "a former prostitute, her old man is in the Santé and she lives alone with her little girl."

Annie, ex-whore.... A madam? A trick? I sort of have cold feet.

No: she's neither one nor the other. She is ugly, with a clear-cut, angular, stunning ugliness; her head is rather horsey, her body gangling under a cheap, ruffled housecoat; her slippered feet are long, her legs suggest elegance. She is as tall as Julien, and Julien subsides: of course you have to look embarrassed, the package is getting more and more cumbersome. I hadn't been carried over Annie's threshold like a giddy wife who'd gone and hurt herself; I'd climbed the stairs all alone, on my three legs, trying not to stumble on the dark, unfamiliar steps, following Julien who was carrying the suitcases. Now, my bags are sitting in front of the stove, blocking the hallway; we are standing, enormous in this tiny room.

"Here, Anne," Annie says, "take the armchair, you'll be more comfortable. Would you like a stool, to rest your foot on? But sit down, Julien! Good heavens, you act like you didn't know the place.... Excuse me, I don't have anything to drink, I'll send Nounouche out. Nounouche!" she calls, leaning out of the window, almost touching the tree, the large tree that has grown, like an explosion, in the gray and suffocated courtyard of this building.

Nounouche doesn't answer.

"She's off again playing around on the boulevard," her mother says.

Julien rummages in the beach bag and pulls out a bottle, my nighttime friend:

"The kid just has brandy, but it's only five o'clock, after all."

Annie gets out glasses, we have a drink, and then she shows me around the apartment: we'll be living in a very small space, there are only two rooms. Perhaps the cramped quarters will help us get along better than the desert of the roadhouse....

"You'll sleep in Nounouche's bed, she'll sleep with me. I've cleared a shelf in the closet for your things, make yourself at home."

Seated on the child's bed separated from the double bed by a foot of space, I let heat and listlessness flood over me before smiling and picking myself up. The closet touches the foot of my bed, the window is right beside the closet, and to look into the courtyard you have to squeeze in between the closet and the table. I inhale Paris, I'm hiding in her heart, I've come back. Beaten, broken, I'm here all the same; furthermore, as we often said in jail, the winner is the one who gets away. I'm coming back, Paris, with what's left of me, to start to live and fight again.

A certain disorder—intimate, familiar, Nounouche's toys and shoes, scattered clothes—binds the objects and the furniture together.

I empty the suitcase onto the shelf, then I go back into the other room, bebopping: here there are no agonizing spaces, you just have to hang onto something and haul yourself along, I won't need my crutches except to go outdoors. Annie and Julien are talking; I, I post myself at the edge of the window, my nose in the tree: the courtyard comes and goes, chatters, children ran, hopscotch squares are drawn; laundry is drying, splotching and blinding the windows.

This time, I'm to be Annie's grandniece, come to rest at her place after an automobile accident. I come from "the provinces," it's big and vague, it doesn't interest Parisians.

"... anyhow," Annie says, "I never visit with anyone. As for my husband, they know or they don't know, I don't care: good morning, good night. There is old Mrs. Villon, at the end of the hall: she makes ready-to-wear clothes at home—things to order too, it depends on the price. Since her kids go to school with mine, of course I have to pay her a little call from time to time. Or else, it's she who comes with her husband, on Sunday, for a game of cards; but outside of that ... since I've been alone, I don't go out of the house anymore, it disgusts me to go out. Shopping, the visits on Saturday, delivering my ties, and that's all."

Her ties?...

Talking all the while, Annie goes back to her work: she snatches a tie from the back of her chair, behind her, and a piece of quilting from the bundle nestled against her stomach; she stretches the tie out on one knee, tightly folded; and with big basting stitches, her large needle runs from one end of the tie to the other, attaching the quilting as it goes. Annie knots the thread, opens her knees, freeing the tie which falls to the floor, rethreads the needle, catches up the next piece of work.... I wonder how many tie-hours must be completed to earn the equivalent of ten minutes of her ex-profession. Julien spoke to me about a certain bet about fidelity ... but all the same, this genteel work doesn't square at all with the way she talks and the style she affects. Anyhow, I reserve judgment and declare to Annie that I'm thrilled to have her for my aunt. She laughs, and keeps on sewing without a pause, picking up after each knot and before the next rethreading, her cigarette, resting on the big box of matches beside the pack, the ashtray, the scissors, the glass: the little necessary implements. And the slipper advances on the stool, moving the knee, the tie falls, the pile grows.... I feel dizzy, I am ashamed of my inaction:

"Can I help you?"

"You see," says Julien, "the power of example! Do you hire help, Annie?"

"I hire, I fire.... Look: now they have to be turned right side out—with that curtain rod, there. Then, I tie them up by the dozen, put them in the suitcase...."

"Without pressing them?"

"Before tying them up, I press the collar seams a little, to flatten them, but the final pressing, that's my brother-in-law's department. Yes, I fill in between two in-laws! My husband's sister does the seams and the hems by machine, I sew them, I hand them back, they finish them. Of course, for them, it pays a lot more than for me. Ah! If I only had a machine and could be on my own...."

(Julien, come on and "find" a machine!)

Up until dinnertime, we make pleasant and insubstantial plans, gathered around a pile of unfinished neckties. Annie is exploited by her in-laws, that's obvious; she can have a clear conscience about anything else, providing there is anything else.... Shut up, Anne, don't start imagining things.

"... especially since they're more and more casual about everything," Annie continues. "They tell me to bring the delivery at three o'clock, for instance, and they get back at five, and I cool my heels drinking Ricard waiting for them.... Speaking of Ricard, I'll go down and get some, it will give me a chance to get Nounouche back home. What can you expect, she has to let off steam, and around here there's no room."

She goes into the bedroom and returns, wearing a dress. She rinses out a glass with water from a pitcher on the dresser, takes her wallet out of the drawer. Julien stops her:

"But, since Anne will be going around in the neighborhood anyhow, why don't all three of us go down to the bar?"

"No, some other time.... It's more relaxed, here. On evenings when it's too quiet, I turn up the radio a little: like this, like I was eavesdropping, buzz buzz. The bar is O.K. when you have nothing to talk to yourself about."

Talk to yourself about!...

"She seems nice," I say to Julien as soon as we are alone. "I like it here: I think it will be all right.... She's certainly a good sort, and.... Good Lord! Four years, her Jules? I pity her. How much does be have left to do?"

"He must be getting into his third year. But ... don't get carried away: Annie's a very good kid, as you say, but above all she's very tough. So, just keep pretending you're a dope, you see nothing, you know nothing. She's paid up for two months: eat, and don't break your ass. She'll tell you stories, true or false: believe them all. And ... anyhow don't jazz around too much in Paris."

"I'll make ties all day long, I promise. There doesn't seem to be much else to do.... What frightens me the most, is the kid!"

The door opens and a little blond cataclysm moves in on us. Once in front of the dresser, Nounouche brakes and cries out:

"Hey, Julien! How's it going?"

Nounouche must be seven or eight years old. She's already an old maid, of a pallor mottled with pink spots and freckles, the brush of a ponytail sweeps her shoulders: she looks like an unripe apricot, warmed over by the Paris sun. She speaks with frankness and authority, is familiar with everyone, she is gracious and charming, already feminine: she has scaled Julien's knees and talks to him gravely, nestled like a lover against his jacket.

Annie comes back in, carrying the glass full of pastis:

"Nounouche, get down from there, you're a nuisance. Go and get some cold water out in the hall."

"No."

"Yes."

"Then I want to have a drink too."

"O.K., O.K.," Annie says.

I hear the faucet running in the hall: there is no running water in the apartment. You wash and do the cooking in a kitchen-closet; Annie shows me the pail, the washbasin, the place where I could put my toilet articles:

"And when you wash, lock the door, because with my daughter around ..."

I have the feeling that I'll have to gag her down somehow, that apricot.

9

Within a week, I have exhausted every *Intimité* and *Nous* in Annie's library, and if I've read *Confidences*, I've heard some too. I clearly have no talent for tie-making, and Annie won't hear of my helping her with the dishes or the cooking:

"With your leg, don't even think of it!"

So, I go walking along the boulevard. I go along, dragging my foot like a turtle lugs its shell, with the same methodical slowness. Summer makes the shadows tremble in the chestnut trees; there, at the end, in the oasis of the intersection. I don't make it: I turn back and go home docilely, just when I said I would. The eye of my conscience is the face of a watch. If Annie gets back from making her deliveries one or two hours late, that's her affair; but I ... I am still ruled by the clock, the clock of others who are afraid of my absences, the invisible prison clock that watches you and brings you back; but then, at Annie's, I don't feel so much like escaping.

"A little more wine, Anne? You know, it's only ten per cent alcohol, not very dangerous...."

At night, after dessert, we talk until the bottle's finished. Annie and I: two women, deprived of love and splendor: I can't, she doesn't want to anymore. All day, we are bound together, linked by the similarity of gestures, of menus, of the sufferings of women, by the needles moving simultaneously, hers to the left, mine to the right: our chairs face each other and I am left-handed, we mirror each other. We sew, we smoke, we hum; from time to time we smile at each other, sighing.... But it's during the evening that we become completely intimate. The camaraderie of the workshop is put aside, neatly relegated among the ties, packed up in the work suitcase; and intimacy is woven, thread by thread, glass by glass, across the table where we preside, among the wax flowers and the piled-up plates.

Nounouche runs between us, climbs up on our knees, cleans up the crumbs and the ashtray, buzzes over our whispers.

"Come on, Nounouche, to bed!" Annie says without conviction at the end of every quarter-hour after eight o'clock.

In front of this minuscule listener, it's important to talk unintelligibly: Annie wants her girl to "stay a little girl," talks to her about Santa Claus, about cabbages and roses; she almost assaulted Madame Villon when the latter, wanting to undertake Nounouche's sexual education along with that of her own girls, showed her some pictures in the medical *Larousse*; but she sees nothing wrong in letting her stay up with us until midnight: she'll sleep late the next morning. When she goes to school.... Anyhow, what do you think she can understand, come now! Your father is in the hospital as you can see for yourself every Saturday, you must believe your mother: and no one else, if the neighbors say something you just have to answer that they are dopes and we are a bunch of bums.

So runs Annie's pedagogy. I especially admire the infallibility and the sure authority that she attributes to herself in the face of everything that Nounouche sees, hears, and registers.

"Watch out, Anne," Nounouche tells me, "your husband will go to the hospital too, if he's naughty. Anyhow, your husband ... think of it! At your age! ..."

And, when rye successfully finished a tie:

"Hey, mama? That's not bad, for her age?"

It's impossible to get her to admit that I'm not a kid like herself; I have to kiss Teddy every night, and in between meals eat from her little tea set. The bear has passed, back and forth through the gates of the Santé Prison; the little tea set has perhaps encountered, in the corridors of the big prison, other bits of tin, mess plates, or keys: on Saturdays, Nounouche accompanies her mother to the bedside of her poor sick father, and she never forgets to bring one or another of her toys, so that Papa, from behind his grille, can play for a half an hour.

I don't like to go with them; it's not that it depresses me, but visiting hours are the only moments in the week when I have the joint to myself. Aimlessly, and even without curiosity I rummage through everything, to make up for the six other days of "Annie, is it all right if I ..."; I wash my hair; I can look at myself in the mirror through the bathroom door which opens directly onto the bedroom and closet doors: Eve again, wearing nothing but an after-shampoo towel, I move through a desert strewn with ties and toys. To prove my good will and erase all trace of my discoveries—the disgrace of a pile of dirty laundry stuffed in a ball between the stove and the gas meter, the sadness of a piece of cheese forgotten for months at the back of the cupboard—I polish the floor and the bottoms of the pots; I put things away without encroaching on the mess too much, settling for giving it a more geometric look; and, in my impatience to see them again, I go down and get some candy at the store, two double Ricards at the bar, and I prepare to welcome them. All the same, I'd sort of like to go some day and hang around outside Chez Marcel, on rue de la Santé, across from the prison. The faces on that street belong to people who aren't allowed to visit, friends of the relatives of an inmate; the packages and suitcases piled all over the place are for the prisoners or come from them: they contain their clean or dirty laundry, perhaps they conceal the file or the dough for the escape of the century.... No: at Marcel's every face is honest, and all traffic as well.

I'd watch the people and packages coming and going, clean and happy, dirty and sobbing; and the view from the wings of the great prison would touch me, as when I fondle Julien's empty shirts.

Annie's in-laws also have visiting rights and never fail to show up: so husband and brother play host together, since the inmate who plays both roles can only have one visit a week. The wife, the sister, the brother-in-law: I only get one side of the picture—Annie's—but I'm sure the other must be just as impassioned about the conflicting truths and lies. Brotherly duty, brotherly anathema, brotherly hatred. But, there is only one means of transportation to the man who stirs up all these feelings: the brother-in-law's car.

Saturdays, at about one, it is I who make the family coffee: Annie, for fear of spoiling her appearance, won't lift a finger until she gets back from the visit. All morning, hour by hour, I've watched emerging from the bathrobe and curlers a harlot: from skinny, her legs become ethereal, through the arch of the very high heels, the tightness of the slit skirt; the cut of the suit rounds the hips, breaks the angular line of the buttocks. The hair begins to fluff out and shine, the lips grow full and pink, making the teeth seem smaller; with rapid little strokes of the mascara brush, the eyes are ringed with a languorous lushness.

But for all that, the brother-in-law doesn't change his line of patter: if he hands out any compliments, it's I who receive most of them. He doesn't flirt with me, he's as aware of his bulk as of the respect due nieces-in-law; but his eyes blink over heavy and schematic thoughts. Eyes black as coffee, contracted by the enormous lenses for his myopic eyes, distant, very beautiful. Luckily the glasses hide them a little, they don't go with the rest of him: a doll's nose squashed between bulging cheeks, fat all over, hairy hands, the ox is an ox, a giant slug, a sea lion swimming in a sea of Pernod. Annie tells me:

"Pew, he talks, and talks, but that's all he can do. After Dédé's arrest, I couldn't come back here right away: they'd sealed the door and besides, I wanted to wait until the thing had blown over a little.... So, I went and spent a few weeks with them. Well, my dear ..."

During her stay, Annie had seen some far from brilliant things: for him, "you'd have to use a snail holder," she, she goes on sprees and buys herself things all the time; as for their daughter, Pat, she's half-dead from work and, at twenty, has drooping breasts and a hunched back.

It's the family, the bond, the ball and chain; but in the end, one has to earn a living.

I get paid myself: as little and as badly as I sew, I earn enough to pay my way. I also buy a few clothes, gradually putting Ginette's in the rag pile.

"Aha! We may get drunk but at least we're all dressed up!" cries the sister-in-law.

Abandoning our practical housecoats, we've gotten rigged out almost as sumptuously as on Saturdays, to attend the family lunch. They invite us every week, we accept one out of three times: convention.

Their house is located at the end of the paved roads of Paris, where the mud and the little anemic gardens begin: we have to take buses, change, walk along streets lined with fences, with walls, with grilles; my leg jerks, Annie trips along on her spikes, Nounouche drags her shoes in the bottom of the gutter whining: "Hey Mama? Are we almost there?"

We get there: the house is all of white wainscoting pierced with bay windows, bored through by airy staircases spiraling from floor to floor; the interior is a network, a forest of neckties. Ties have built the walls, step by step, light night after gray day when the whole family, crammed into two rooms in the Temple Quarter, cut, sewed, ironed and hemmed, stitched and pinned without cease; the ties followed the move and immediately reasserted their rights. Here they serve as upholstery, as pillows, as ornaments. The ties have only spared the kitchen: the family necessities are of equal importance—to work and to eat. Not all the rooms are furnished yet: going to wash my hands in the tiny bathroom, I notice the bidet, which has been delivered wrapped in strips of brown paper and stands, thus mummified, in a corner.

These Sundays when I am left out, in spite of the syrupy welcome of the tie-making gentry, I play with Nounouche in the little garden, I don't talk, I'm bored. I am a stranger to their past, their present, and their future; Annie and I, tie manufacturers, while waiting for Dédé, released, to resume the building trade and construct two twin residences to shelter us two couples, oh yes, those plans fill our evenings, but here ... what is there to say? This Sunday exists, gray and blabbering: you have to get through it like the Sundays at Central, mouth closed and smiling, ears open and cheerful; the difference being that here chicken with rice, with peppers, with peas, or potatoes replaces the beef pot roast, stew, or hash.

The Pernod, the smoke, the chicken, the voices all mingle and weigh on my heart, I am alone, heavy, far away. When will I be able to walk, to get away from these people once and for all? My presence doesn't bother them: Julien makes suit of that, pays some more for my board, and goes off. I hide my ingratitude, my ill temper, my constant deception: how much more I liked my buddies in the *Série Noire!* Since my escape, I've only hung around ex-prisoners, those recaptured and not recaptured by the law; of course, as a prelude to meeting up with Rolande again, I hadn't intended to see any other kinds of people, I dreamed of unsavory relations, unsavory: acts, of a whole lot of unsavory things to parade in front of her; but my dreams are ending, summer is ending. Rolande is becoming unreal.... Hello, it's me: you see, I've come. What can you, what do you want to do with me, tomorrow, after we've eaten, drunk, talked, and slept together? Do you believe that I still care about making pilgrimages to your ass, now that other ways of coming and crying are known to me? Between you and me, with every second, time is running out; I remain in darkness, but if somewhere there is a dawn and I find the way to it, I'll walk there without leaning on you, Rolande, Rolande I'll be damned if it's your fault that my leg is busted, yes: I would have gotten out in any case, I would have met Julien anyhow, and I would not be obliged to think of you today, my sweet, with gratitude and rancor in my heart. I don't know if I still like women and despise men; but the man to like, the woman to despise, I know their names ... Julien ... but ... I love you! ...

Julien, I don't want to sound confused, I close my mouth with your kisses; but I know that the time has come, that I can no longer fool around at the crossroads, that I must choose one path, oh, Rolande, Julien, I am torn in two. ...

At Central, we divided our Sundays between dancing and playing cards. Cards were torture for me: once trump had been played, I lost interest in the game. I observed the play of hands, their grace or clumsiness in holding the cards, the surprised or impassive expression of the eyes. All the same, I really liked the ace of clubs, "the triumph" in card language: two or three clovers turned up in the same day meant that we would succeed at everything. ... Yes, it was time for me to escape: the club, the benzine, the poison of twisted dreams, the onanism, and the whole prison were leading me straight to Saint Anne's. I am still, each day further, escaping madness. ...

Annie owns three decks of cards, of which two are incomplete and worn out by the games Nounouche plays with her dolls on Sundays, at the feet of the grownups who are playing above her on the table; to steal the ace of clubs from her wouldn't spoil the meaning of the game much, Nounouche plays at mimicry more than at cards. I will put the Triumph in an envelope and send it to Rolande. If I end up dropping her anyhow, too bad: I would have warned her. If I seemed a little sluggish that night, it would simply be because the date chosen is also the date of my birthday. Twenty years old, a new decade, my poor present, and the certitude of going back to spend a part of it in jail: the remainder of that sentence I interrupted for you, my rejected present!

"Say Julien, will you come, for my twentieth birthday?"

"If I can, gladly: we'll go and have dinner somewhere...."

"Oh, Annie can perfectly well make something for us. We'd have to invite her too and, if we're going out, I'd rather be alone with you."

We start to figure out my future: to stay here, first of all, Julien will guarantee the means, I won't take any chances, no, that's a promise.... I think it over, miserable: I'm tired of accepting favors. Since Annie is my treasury and I don't want to sour her by exterior signs of wealth, if Julien gives me ten thousand I declare five of them and slip two and a half into her kitty, for the Ricards and Nounouche's candies. Later, when I'm able to walk better ...

But is it really true that I walk so badly?...

They've taken off my cast, on two occasions. For the first checkup I'd removed the sneakers and the elastic bandage; I'd envisioned myself, feeling my way along, on Julien's arm, like a new girlfriend; I "unveiled" my foot in dreams, pretending to walk again at night, pushing against the sheet with my toes; to speed things along, I'd even taken off my cast the night before the visit.

I borrowed the tie scissors, the big ones, and I started to cut, below the kneecap: I was going to cut the plaster either side of the leg, as I'd seen done at the hospital, lift the cover, and take my leg out of its case, delicately, like taking a soufflé out of the oven ... alas! At the end of a half-hour I'd just barely made a notch of a fraction of an inch; a little gritty dust dirtied the linoleum where I was sitting, at Annie's feet, so I could give her the scissors at the end of each tie and take them back: at that rate, I might as well wait for an electric saw.

I then had the idea of melting the plaster: I soaked my leg in a bucket of hot water, and I unwound, unwound ...

It was so ugly, under there, that I put on a sock and didn't even try to walk.

During the consultation I was given, along with an elaborate bawling-out, a new cast, called a "walking" cast. Lying on the table of the bandaging room, I saw my leg disappear again for yet another stretch of time.

"And try to keep this one on," the doctor finished, "or else you won't walk for the next ten years."

While be was talking, he was checking the thickness of the heel—a cube of gauze which was hardening rapidly, while an aide gave a quick cleaning to my toes and knee which were smeared with plaster.

My foot was going to do again what it had been made to do: place itself in front of the other foot, support for a second the entire weight of the body ... and I had walked for such a long time without even thinking about it! I was about to know the joy of parents at the first steps of their child, augmented by my own joy; to advance without being propped up like a walking doll, neither being pushed nor pulled.... Julien was waiting for me on the wooden bench, with the other patients who were waiting their turn, and the woman in white who was waiting for noon behind her switchboard; and I, I was through with waiting, I was turning my back, my hands finally free, on those months of shut-in pain; in the doorway of the waiting room I smiled, hesitant, I would have liked to run to Julien, to be light, to surprise him ... but this cast was heavy, much heavier than the crutches, and it was he who came to me to hold me up, under the elbow this time, supporting each of my grotesque steps.

Annie lent me a cane with a rubber tip, and I started going about on three legs again, like a windmill, on pins and needles.

And now?

I plant myself in front of the closet, my back to the mirror, I twist my neck around to observe my ankles, I walk over to the kitchen door: no, it's not possible, I'm not limping, I don't see or feel myself limping. I don't have enough room to run, but the old bursts of speed are stirring in my calves; I can't hop, or eyed balance myself on my new pin, but I'll will it so strongly that I'll succeed.

"... Give me that cigarette: you smoke in the street, and then what next? Do you absolutely insist on calling attention to yourself?"

Julien is freshly shaved, his shirt crackles, his hair is parted in a thousand places, the furrows of a wet comb: he is never without his toilet kit, and a stopover during the day provides him with water and a mirror. This morning he arrived pale with fatigue, bluish circles beneath his eyes; he slept on my little bed, rolled up in his duffle coat, a stone, dead, deaf to my plans:

Since I'm getting around and staying awake more, I'm learning what it's like to be tired again, I feel soft tinglings, at night under my eyelids; but this brutal, knocked-out way of falling asleep, this need more imperious than hunger or thirst, the binds and kidnaps.... If I have to go into the room, no need to enter carefully, I can go from tiptoeing to banging my heels on the floor and jostle the bed and hum and sing and shout: Sleep is stronger than I am.

"Put out that butt...."

I miss that little while back, Julien, when you were sleeping, deaf but also dumb: I could lean over you, pass my hands in front of your face, pinch you, strangle you; now, I am your clumsy thing, your rabbit, your little girl, you look at me with decision and you talk like a man! I know: later, on the boulevard, your arm will get rounder, more helping, it will be a grip, a refuge for me, and your steps will wait for mine; we'll take taxis, we'll go into bars....

"What would you say to a drink?"

My parents only had a drink once or twice a year, at the bar in the station when we were traveling, or when we were showing guests around the city and had to refresh their feet and their throats. Some syrup for the little one. I would suck on my grenadine, sprawl out against the high, caned back, in the bustle of the terrace; I would ask to go to the bathroom to take in the atmosphere, the neon and the glitter of the bar, to touch the big egg of soap that turned on its chromium axis ... later the *brasseries* become bars and night clubs: I cram my nights into them, my idleness and thirst, I talk and smoke until daylight drives me out, and from time to time I disentangle myself to put on a record and dance to it.

However, no bar ever served as my waiting room for more than ten minutes: I was punctual and wanted others to be the same.

But when Julien tells me "I'll be right back" and comes back one or two hours later, what can I do but wait for him with one eye on the door? Where to go, where return, unless to Annie's in a while in the final taxi? I empty my glass, I'm thirsty, I call the waiter, before the fresh glass I bite into another chunk of patience. My sense of reality, the proof that Julien has really been there, are, the mornings after going out with him, the circle of alcohol around my temples, and that pleasant heaviness in the upper parts of my legs.... Julien has slept in the little bed, but he has said good-bye to Annie the night before, so as not to have to wake her; it's still dark when I get up to follow him into the dining room, heat up the water and make coffee: no, no use bothering, Julien has already washed with cold water, he'll get some coffee at the station; Julien has changed moods, he has left the lovemaking in the warmth of the pillow, and I relock the door on his haste: well, *ciao*, excuse me, I'm late, I'm going to miss the train.

One or two weeks of being alone, now.

"My little rabbit, I cheated on you!" he says sometimes on arriving.

And I answer, smiling:

"I hope it was good, was it?"

The road is as bare and harsh as a desert: later, perhaps, calmly, we'll start down magic pathways.... From now until then there is still a great deal of pain, a great many people and things to annihilate: thread by thread I unravel, I destroy; I hate myself for making a "project" out of Julien, but I sense too many false and sticky attachments around him, these at least I would like to break off.

I used to be pampered, petted, fussed over, too, in the old days: I was intact and able to bite, my cupboard was full and my claws were ingenious.

My equipment was destroyed, I am wounded and begging, and it's I now who offers herself and clings; people don't hold onto me at all, for I have nothing to give them but myself, myself naked, and it will take a lot of time and tenderness before some resource, some source springs up in me.

10

"Oh, Annie …"

It's hard to get out:

"When you're buying your butts, would you mind picking up a pack for me?"

In her pants which accentuate her skinny hips, with her penciled eyebrows and woolly hair, Annie is an incongruity: she has the top of an old doll and the bottom of a teenager. In the market, she causes a sensation. So, I avoid going with her.

Later, when she comes back, balanced by her two string bags of groceries, I'll light up the last stump of my last Gitane, to get the unpacking started without seeming too eager about it. Actually, I've been broke since last night: my budget got wrecked when I bought some *apéritifs* to drink with Julien, who had promised to stop by and didn't come. What happened to him?

Annie, opening the door, interrupts my thought and puts it into words:

"Oh, dear, what a sad little girl, this morning! Well, anyhow,

I got enough grub for the week, at least we won't starve for a while. But after that ..."

She talks confusedly about borrowing from Villon "who always lets you know it when *she* needs something," about touching her sister-in-law, etc., all this to get around to asking me to persuade Julien, when he's alone with me of course, to give her a little advance on next month's board.

She's too much, that one!

I explain that Julien is not my client, that it's not his dough I love and that he doesn't owe us a thing: today's the 23rd. It's not my fault if Annie goes to the hairdresser and buys new clothes for Nounouche and sends packages to Dédé. And she comes crying to me, who has nothing left in the world except one Gitane butt, until she unpacks the groceries! Sitting, with the needle in my fingers, knees gripping the tie, my eyes are on a level with her waist and I spot the rectangle of the pack of butts bulging in her pocket. I think of the warmth of the smoke which flows, liquid, with a slight bitter edge, into your throat and chest, making your blood tingle; I think of all the ashtrays I've emptied in my life; tortured by my craving, I sit there, unable to care about what Annie's saying, my eyes riveted on her pants.

"It's not enough just to have it, you have to know how to spend it": Pierre. "You just wait, if I ever really put myself out ...": Pedro. "Don't get all worked up, Anne, I'll get hold of some": Annie. Among these impalpable fortunes built of words and wind, Julien has nothing else except money. Money, it's necessary and natural, it's air and blood, so why talk about it?

"But Annie, you still have one week of board money left, don't you?"

"You don't realize how much things cost, I swear! Come shopping a little more often, you'll see!"

"Impossible: I'm sure to come back with four wallets instead of one. But ... you're right, I'll go and do a little window-shopping, to get an idea."

I've got a head full of cotton, cotton that winds and contracts into a tighter and tighter ball. I need to walk around Paris, to find again the odor of streets in the morning, the passages through the market in the jostling of baskets; perhaps I'll go beyond the neighborhood, the shabbily dressed women and the workmen wavering in their blues, I'll come upon spotless streets, in the depths of the city....

"You're taking Nounouche?"

(Shit!...)

"If she wants.... We'll go to the carousel horses.... I feel like seeing Luco...."

"Well, Nounouche? Do you want to go with Anne?"

"No. I don't feel like going out. I'm staying with *my mother*."

Her good little jealous, filial heart shows me the door: all right.

This is the first time I've walked in Paris outside the limits of Annie's boulevard in years. I stop at the intersection: the policeman, the pedestrian crossings, the métro, and beyond, the maze of houses and streets, to infinity. If I cross this boundary, if I plunge underground or if I go on to the next boulevard, how will I bring myself to go back to Annie, her lousy coffee, her footstool for making ties, Annie of the Santé Prison, Annie of the Boulevard Sebastopol?

But I have to keep Annie, in order to keep Julien: I'm beginning to recognize all the people Julien describes, but I don't know one address, not one name that isn't either a nickname or a pseudonym, I have no way to find him. Except Annie.

Julien parts the fog for an instant. I penetrate it with him, my lips dry; then he vanishes, I turn back to the colorless day, looking for what he took away with him and where I no longer can go.

I lean on the railing of the métro to count my change: it's all right, I have enough to buy a ticket.

When I get back up into the fresh air again, every detail of the neighborhood hits me in the eye, instantly familiar: these stores, I know every window of them, every sign in big or little letters, I know which ones gleam in the solitude of winter streets, walking at night. The years roll back, I am sixteen, I am scuffing my shoes along the sidewalk; and like that, with my hair loose and my breasts naked under my sweater, like the gypsy in the advertisements for Gitanes I am walking on clouds. Paris caresses me with a thousand looks, it offers itself as I offer myself:

"Now see here, I'm a free person, aren't I? Go on, go away, I tell you."

"Come now, bad French girl, why be a meanie?"

Oh yes, the Arabs are still here too, eyes benign and heavy with honey, and the confident "Walk ahead, I'll follow you," and the big and little old men, guys all dressed up and guys in working clothes. What a difference between them and these, the ones today who walk beside, in front of and behind me, whispering: "Would you like to have a drink?"

We'd have a drink, we'd put down our glasses, we'd be back in ten minutes.... I no longer know how, I no longer dare.

One of my drinking companions would make a sign, sometimes, from behind his Calvados: we would look at the people on the heated terrace, the crowd that was gradually forming in front of the door: men walking back and forth a couple of yards in either direction, a little saraband within the main one. "I think someone's waiting for you," my friend would say, "I won't keep you...."

My escorts from the past regroup now, they surround me. But I walk without slowing down, my eyes on the ground, I am frightened. Supposing one of them's a cop, supposing ... Come on, Anne, raise your eyes, choose, get on your back one more time....

"Just for a short while?" asks the floor maid, who has not recognized me.

The lock. The shedding of intimate garments, the pause: oh yes, your little present, is that it? It is indeed.

I am absent, submissive, I don't think about anything. I won't even be late for lunch.

And my eyes will never be riveted to Annie's pockets again.

Besides, the next morning I catch her red-handed without meaning to; she's sending Nounouche to buy the bread, gives her a thousand franc bill saying:

"And be careful not to lose it, it's the last one."

Nounouche goes back to rummage in the room.

"What on earth are you doing?" cries Annie.

"Just a minute, Mama, I'm getting my doll...."

And she appears amid our piles of ties, one hand waving the handle of her doll's traveling bed, the other a five thousand franc bill:

"And this one, Mama, you couldn't remember where you'd hidden it?"

What a scene! Nounouche, her bottom black and blue, her mouth open and howling; Annie, pale with rage, out of breath from so much spanking and trying to explain to me the origin ("small amounts saved up from her earnings") and destination ("Dédé's Christmas present") of the hoard so calamitously unearthed.

After that, I become a big spender: I buy whatever I please, I come home laden with packages, cakes, bottles, useful supplies: laundry soap, canned goods.... And Annie doesn't question me and balances her budget very nicely, besides: no more problem about using me to hit Julien. So, we sweetly dupe each other, she praising the generosity of her in-laws, I that of my friend.

However, certain coldnesses, certain remarks irresistibly blurted out and immediately taken back with a smile, make me feel that the atmosphere is deteriorating beyond a hope of patching it up. For instance, during the first weeks, when Julien would come, Annie would play the warm hostess, with calm and maternal discretion; if Julien wasn't going to spend the night, she would make herself scarce over at the Villons, taking the cards and a bottle of wine:

"Come on, let's go, Nounouche.... Have a good time, kids, we'll be back in about an hour."

We should have rivaled her in delicacy, not touched the bed, caressed each other with precaution; but we preferred to spread out all over the place, smoke near the bed of the child who had bronchial trouble, empty the bottles Julien brought without leaving a drop for the good-bye toast when, later, the intruders would come home. And for us the hour would stretch out, long, far, back to the last evening, ahead to the next—if it were to be given to us to live another one. The bonds would strengthen, night and fear would go away, Julien's fingers would pass over me, balm and fire.... I would have the impression of making love in jail, menaced by a Judas, laid out on a very small surface and in a very short space of time a pool, an island of time. Then we would erase all the traces of our escapade, remaking the bed, our faces, our attitudes. Really! Annie's apartment, her sheets, the utensils she used with Dédé.... In the beginning, I used to admire her, I would sympathize with her:

"Me, filled with you, and Annie, the poor thing..."

Julien would laugh, secretly:

"Don't you worry about her...."

After that five thousand franc note, I've stopped worrying.

It was on the night of my twentieth birthday, over champagne, after the toasts, that my stay with Annie entered its period of open disintegration. I hadn't peeped about this birthday for a long time; and Annie, who only reads the calendar backward—"Still so-and-so many days for Dédé" had luckily forgotten the date. But Julien must have jotted it in his engagement book, that reminder blackened all over with words and signs that he consults ceaselessly: at eight o'clock he arrived, followed by my chauffeur from May, and both of them smothered me with flowers, with boxes, with kisses, and with good wishes.

"Oh, gladiolas.... But they're as big as me! Thank you...."

They put them in a jar, on the floor, behind my chair: I was posed against this background like a fashion photograph; they cut the only candle in the house in half, one piece for each decade. But we didn't know that, in terms of the well-imitated friendship that had made us bear with each other until then, this meal would be the last. Nounouche placed ladyfingers beside each plate, like at a fancy tea; the friend had gone, Annie was yawning into her glass and my twenty years already had a dent in them, sliding second by second toward the twenty-first, the longed-for, the major, the momentous year.

The girls went to bed: "And be sure and bolt the door," Annie said mechanically, kissing me one last time. Julien, thus dismissed from my bed, didn't want to stay with me, nor take me somewhere else, nor rent a hotel room under an assumed name; he granted none of my wishes, and we unnerved each other so with the dregs of the bottles and the battle of words, trying to build for ourselves and banging our heads against the blind wall of impossibles, that I ended by getting a slap and returning it:

"Oh, Julien," I sobbed, "I love you...."

"Me, I only love my mother...."

That's how we agreed, finally, to recognize and to believe that we loved each other.

Now, those words, in the secret of my memory, make me laugh and move farther and farther away: I love, the star is born. Rolande must have received the ace of clubs; everything is virginal, luminous, a shining unknown invites my steps. Just a little more patience.... But how to leave Annie? What occasion or quarrel drum up?

The invalid's armchair, in the dining room, has become a lovers' chair: we don't want anything more from the little bed. Or else, I introduce Julien to the hotels of my youth. Those moments, when our bodies and our hearts play and rest one on the other, bring back other "moments," spent before with other men: without shame, without lying, I relate them, like strange or fictional stories; the past throws off sparks, then goes out and cauterizes itself.

—May nothing tarnish this instant....

And we plunge back into the streets, we drag along, we dawdle; here anyhow is the boulevard, the apartment house, the courtyard. Annie is fixing supper, Nounouche looks for candy in our pockets. We all three look at each other with false smiles, we let the radio speak, having nothing to say to each other; to occupy our mouths, we smoke and drink until it's time for "Good night, kids, and be sure and bolt the door, Anne."

Tonight, finally, the joint explodes.

We'd brought up a bottle, from the bar of the hotel where we'd spent the afternoon; on top of that, we'd already had a lot to drink; we got to Annie's during dessert.

Nounouche, for once, has remembered her mother's lesson and applies herself to not looking at us, forgetting to sulk over her plate which she empties, bite by bite; Annie swallows with her customary appetite, only opening her mouth to stuff something into it. Our places are not set. Tired of standing in front of the buffet, I decide to escape the humiliation that this staging must logically provoke, and go to bed. I navigate the entire length of the room with relative dignity; and there my toe, catching on a roughness in the linoleum or tangled in a tie, slips under me and pulls me down, as the décor capsizes and the alcohol bursts in my ears. Annie starts to jeer:

"Well, you're a pretty sight, both of you! Since that's the way it is, it's going to change: I want you to know, Julien, that my house is not a brothel, and that ..."

Suddenly I recover myself, brilliant, cold, rigid:

"I know that, Annie, and that's exactly why I'm not staying here another minute. I'm checking out of the room, and you'll be free to resume your celibate habits and entertain whomever you please. Hey, you, come and help me get my suitcase down from the closet."

Since Julien doesn't budge, I climb up on the foot of my

bed, take down the suitcase, and start throwing in the contents of my dresser. I go into the kitchen, to retrieve my toilet articles, but Annie's shrieks stop me: how interesting is the open heart.

"You are a little whore," she seethes, "a little shit…"

"… a little slut and a little ass," I conclude. "All right, you're finished, may I leave?"

The suitcase is too full, bulging, I can't close it:

"Well, Julien, are you going to help me, yes or no!"

I am the only character in the scene who moves and talks, I feel like kicking them to life, killing, and running away… they just sit there: Annie, in a stupor, recovering from the last waves of her outburst; Julien, immobile, at once attentive and vague. Nounouche, huddled against her mother's chair, cries with little sniffs, outdone for once by this scene, a real serious scene like in the movies, in which tears and the unchained heart take part, tap-tap-tap, poor Nounouche's heart, and me…. I'm beginning to feel utterly infantile. I'm already thinking that it would have been good to drink and talk, again tonight, like three old buddies; Nounouche would be asleep, the suitcase would be in its place on the closet, a promise of leaving, soon, soon…. But I'm sitting on the suitcase, and nothing in the world will make me open it again here: I must leave tonight or never, the occasion is too perfect. Perfect for Julien, patient, irresolute; perfect for me, saturated, ready to throw myself anywhere to do anything. Leave, get back out in the air, sing.

When I get up … here I am up, my forehead resting on Julien's shoulder. I've put my coat on over my suit: it must be cold, under the streetlights of Paris where I will begin to wander again. I do not look at Julien, but I know the absent expression, the pallor, the dark eyes, the moist temples.

"Where are you going, Anne? Where can I find you, now? You're going to get caught ... oh, all that, all that just for this...."

His arms crush me, weld me to him:

"But do you mind so much, really? Aren't you glad I'm getting out of here? We'll be free, see each other as much as we like! No more schedules! No more neckties!"

"I know," he continues. "One is always alone. That was the worst part, you see: that you might leave and that I might never see you again. I'll go on my way. Alone. And never again agree to stop."

Julien, Julien, this water on my cheek, your tears, brief, silent, which knife into my heart.... I laugh, harshly:

"I hope that someday you'll cry as much as I've cried, that you'll wait for me like I've waited for you.... Come on, let's go, now."

"At least tell me where you're going...."

"Never fear, I know where to go. I'll be able to find you too, if you want.... Just tell me where, wherever it suits you, whenever you like. I have nothing else to do: just come at your call, be there, on time, for you."

Julien suggests that we call in Annie, for a reconciliation before I leave ... and to try to arrange it so that I don't leave.

"Tomorrow, I'll get in touch with someone...."

"Another hideout, really! Pierre, Annie, pardon me, but is that how I'm supposed to spend my time on the lam? Listen, Julien: I can walk, go along with you, that's your most wonderful victory...."

Julien misinterprets "go along with you," he thinks that I'm agreeing to stay, closes his eyes and smiles with joy; and I, because of that smile, feel that I'm going to give in.... Just then Annie leaves the room to get some water or go to the bathroom; and her look, punitive and mocking, strengthens my resolution. No, no, I can't stay any longer, I'd either die or kill her.

Dawn is breaking as we leave the apartment, without locking the door. In the taxi to the station, the station where Julien will leave me on the platform, I take his hand: it is cold and lifeless, a dead hand, and his lips are ice cold too.

11

"Don't give up, above all: here she is...."

An indifferent and impatient finger is knocking on the door. I call out "Come in," in the indifferent and unhurried voice of a woman emerging from a sedate night, alone in a hotel bed, and who, habitually, has breakfast brought up to her over which she will fall asleep again, to stretch out the morning. Profession uncertain, identity quite clear, hours regular: the manager is pleased with me and the maids always, find some kind of excuse for the accidents on the sheet. We only spot it with ashes or chocolate: at Nini's and Annie's, Julien and I acquired very discreet habits.... To get up to my room, Julien sneaks past the reception desk while I distract the night watchman with the sound of my key; I meet him on the stairs, I open my door and we rush in as though we were being followed.

That morning my hot plate was busted, and drinking Nescafé with tap water didn't appeal to us. I'd telephoned to order breakfast: one is plenty for two people, with bread and croissants, butter and jam, and a full pot of coffee.

I close the door behind the girl and get Julien out of the bathroom: he is sitting, quietly, on the bidet.

"Come, sweetheart, I'm hungry, hungry...."

The tray on our knees, our gestures short and intermingled, the warm disorder; the ashtray replacing the tray...

"I'll have one more smoke and then cut," Julien says.

"Your train leaves at four past eleven, you said: you have loads of time. Let's go back to sleep for a while."

"No, I've got to see someone. Oh, it's not another girl!..."

What could that matter to me! I bury my nose in Julien's shoulder, I comb his chest with my finger tips; I fill myself with the softness and luster of his skin, I study every detail, every pink or brown speck of him, to be able to remember them and strengthen myself with them until the next happiness: one evening, one night, those are my joys, two or three times a month. The rest of the time, it's just work, drudgery, diffuse fear.

It rains almost every day: my hair frizzes up, my skirt sticks to me in damp folds, my ankle is filled with a heavy, bitter coldness; nevertheless, I walk, I have to. To be able to say to Julien, "Take care of yourself, I'm making out all right," to be vacant and secret, to make him forget those long months when I was dependent on him and the idea that I loved him because I was grateful to him; so that nothing sordid is involved with our encounters, so that it's finally I who worry him and make him miss me a little.... At Pierre's, at Annie's, his affection was at peace, the place was reliable, I was always there; now, I am building a more perilous dwelling, but more habitable, I keep it empty and spacious so I can live in it with him, only keeping for my own use one little corner, the shameful, crowded, messy room.

Later, of course, I'll make "deals," big ones, golden ones, but in the meantime, I have to get by. I never go hungry, but I have a thousand hungers on my mind, and the hunger for Julien which divides itself into a thousand desires, childish, astonishing, complex....

Around four o'clock, I get all dressed up in something that will stay fresh through the evening: run-proof stockings, waterproof mascara, clothes which look elegant but which one is at home in; I fold things and dust them off, I tidy my room like a schoolgirl, first of all because chambermaids scare me a little, secondly because, maybe, I'll never come back to it again.

("Come on, on your feet, no chairs for dames like you, get a load of that broad!")

When after hours of interrogation I might have resigned myself to giving out my address, the cops would find here nothing but a pair of underpants drying on the radiator, and, to safeguard everything too pretty not to seem to them to have been stolen, a sheaf of receipts: a receipt from the post office for the watch, for the traveling iron.

You've got to be prepared for it, at any moment, at every step....

I seldom sleep out: in general, boredom overcomes me long before I can fall asleep, become a shadow, and search for nighttime companions more rewarding than those of the "moment." Anyhow, nights at thirty or fifty thousand francs I only heard about in jail, where the bullshit permits all kinds of grand ideas. Without doubt, a fugitive's nights should be worth more; but night runs into day, every hour has the same color, the pale color of danger. I suppress my fatigue and disgust until I've been paid, then I wash them away in delicious and sound sleep.

In the bars where prostitutes gather, I've run into several minors from Fresnes again, who are hustling on the sly until they're old enough to get their identity card, or who've reached that age and become professionals. In spite of my new image, about fifteen pounds thinner, and my civilian clothes, they've recognized me:

"Oh, Anne! So you're out now?"

I answer that my name isn't Anne, that I'm making my "debut" in Paris, and at the same time I search the rogue's gallery of faces for the gallery on the walls of prison. Gray or brown dresses, thick and cumbersome: the faces of winter; plaid or striped blouses, transparent with age, worn of puffs or pleats: the faces of summer. But, summer or winter, my little sisters would always wear the same mask—pale, mottled or flushed, dark circles under the eyes, and that stale, anonymous, uniform air. At times, one's attention might be caught by more shining eyes, particularly thin lips, or especially white teeth; but how to remember a name, how know from which cocoon these girls emerged, now unrecognizable under a new guise, heavy makeup, tight dresses, dyed hair?

They stay at the bar: they wait for the customer to come to them, they have nothing else to do; they wait, a hip propped against the jukebox, or perched at the bar in front of glasses, as shopkeepers wait at the doors of their shops, hands behind their backs, up there, at the exit from the kingdom of whores, in the network of little streets, in the lighted space of the boulevard. Their take depends on the season, on the way they're dressed or fix their hair:

"Whenever I wear this dress, my dear, I simply never get anywhere."

"I only make out when I'm wearing pants."

Me, I walk. I don't hang around on the street, I don't have the time, I don't like the sidewalk and I don't seem more a whore than anything else. I use this method because it's quick, it requires neither a schedule nor much practice—or so little: I've fended off the paws of pimps, the sneaky tricks of clients since I was sixteen, and nothing much has changed since then.... I'm really only afraid of the cops, having not the slightest identification to show in case they demand it; but I constantly change streets, hotels, my appearance; I sniff passersby before answering them; an obscure but sure intuition stops me or encourages me, signal lights blink in my head, red: watch out, green: it's all right, go ahead, wait, don't wait and get out of here, kid, and fast. I slip through the streets with hurried, determined steps, I hardly limp at all and I walk as quickly as possible: this apparent lack of interest, this kind of "You don't look like the type," serves me as a protection as well as a come-on.

"Can we get together again?"

"Why not, if we happen to run into each other?"

"But come now, where can I find you? You must have someplace, a bar you usually go to?"

"Oh me.... I just keep walking."

To make them happy, when they're particularly generous or pitiful, I make out an itinerary, I jot down a rendezvous in my engagement book—a tentative scribbling for this evening, not leaving anything written lying around, but then, the dope, who does he think he is?—It would be pretty extraordinary if he ever found me again, Paris is a big place. And besides, what do I owe you anyhow? You waited an hour, you say? Well, I waited two hours. That was somewhere else and it wasn't for you, but what does that matter? One of you surely owes me an hour.

Little by little, I get organized, I have a steady income, shopping lists; the joint looks prettier, I'm not getting any uglier, and Julien telephones more often. I won't be caught again, no: the constant thought of Julien conceals and protects me. I don't give a damn about going back to jail, but, today, it would be too absurd ... today is a prelude to another time, a time which will be, itself, a prelude to my capture; but first I want to live a little.... May is almost here: I buy various dresses at the best stores, all different colors; I walk in flats, as before, I get drunk with walking under the budding trees of Easter. It's already a whole year that I've been out!...

Under the words and the caresses of men, I sometimes forget that I'm not as pretty, as nice as all that; if you'd seen me before, you bunch of asses, when I was intact and without love, if you see me tomorrow when I'll be scarred, healed of everything but love ...

As Annie says:

"But you're young.... You think that when we were young, Dédé and I, that everything was a bed of roses?"

To explain my concern about not getting caught and my refusal to get an identity card, I tell the girls that I'm out on probation, on the condition that I don't leave town, you know, and that making the scene alleviates my urge to get the hell out, etc. But the only person in all of Paris who knows the truth is Annie.... So, I made peace almost immediately after my "scene"; and, besides, she had been my mother for more than six months; we had lived through touching, laborious hours together; we had—although for different reasons— both awaited the return of the same man....

The morning when Julien's hands were so cold, the suitcase so heavy, we had lingered in the station restaurant, letting the trains leave; I had asked for some hot chocolate, I didn't have a care in the world, I was starved but full of beans:

"Julien, honey!... Don't look so sad, have some hot chocolate with me.... What are you thinking about? Don't you feel
you can trust me?..."

I jumped off the step just as the last train was leaving; I
carried a telephone number engraved in my head, and this
number unrolled an indestructible cord as the cars went by
me; I held on tightly to this line to save me from doubt and
drowning, at the other end of it I held on to Julien....

In certain parts of Paris, they don't check your identification papers at hotel reception desks: you just have to hand
over an empty wallet with a certain assurance, which the guy
on duty politely hands back. They go by your appearance; and
even if you look lousy, it won't matter at all as long as your
money looks all right.

To begin my life as a free woman opportunely and in grand
style, I slept until evening; after dinner, I went back to bed and
stayed there all the next day. The telephone at the head of my
bed served as my plaything: the hotel bill gave me more lee-
way than putting tokens in a phone booth, I called out several
surprise hellos here and there, and then put in a call to Annie
through the waitress in the bar in her building, the one where
we used to buy drinks by the glass.

Annie accepted my apologies eagerly, apologized back even
more eagerly. "I was a little drunk too, fights just make better
friends anyhow, come and see me soon," etc.

So, from time to time, I show up briefly over there. I bring
packages full of things and, to make amends to Annie's eternal
housecoat for my various outfits (which I'm careful to change
every time I go), I knock myself out with kindness and simplicity. I don't think she'd go so far as to squeal on me, but
I'm frightened and leery of everybody. The thought of getting

arrested never leaves me: I learn to look it in the face, I tame it, I never chase it away. The shadow stalks, I recognize it, I study it, and then I pounce on it: you're coming? Yes, I'm coming. Walk ahead, I'll follow you. From the little guy, the little slip, the disproportionate risk, the aching ankle, the germs and the blows that could strike me down at any moment: protect me, Julien, for it's to you, to you alone that I return. My freedom weighs on me: I would like to live: in a prison where you would know when to open and close the door, a little more, for a little longer time....

I've done pretty well today. I stop to have a drink and a chat with Suzy, an ex-minor who since Fresnes has acquire quite a few pounds and considerable vulgarity, a Jules, and—before the Jules—a little girl who's now three. Her mother sometimes brings her here: while mom's out working she plays behind the bar, or on top of it.

We think back on the times when Suzy—then Suzanne—would be shipped back to Fresnes two or three times a year, for skipping out on the parole officer, petty thefts or vagrancy. Suzanne had the edge, among the minors, because she was almost twenty—real maturity—because she knew how to drive a car, and, even, how to steal one. I look at her, with her chubby hands and fingernails outrageously filed and polished, her milky shoulders showing through her half-lace half-jersey blouse, her very high-heeled shoes which make her feet swell up and end her rounded legs in points. I say:

"By the way, Suzy, what about cars? Are you still crazy about them?"

I imagine her needle heels sliding over the pedals, her fingernails slipping across the leather; I see again Suzanne of Fresnes, whom we would kid after gym class, every noon:

"Get a load of those legs, she really has something to stand on, that girl."

"Oh really!" Suzy says, lighting up her Pall Mall with her silver plated lighter and blowing the smoke up to the ceiling. "Now I've got a kid! I don't touch a thing, I just quietly go about my business...."

And I used to want to get her to put me on to some good deals!

"Two more Ricards, Jojo!" Suzy calls. "One plain and one with mint."

I object: I've really had enough booze for the day.

"Oh come on, this will be the last one!"

"O.K., the last one, then...."

Day before yesterday, Julien appeared behind the wheel of an old car, "a stroke of luck, a real bargain." He showed me the registration, the bill of sale, the insurance policy: certainly the first time I ever heard him boast about having bought something, but undoubtedly he wanted to calm my perpetual tear, don't get all worried, Anne, my pet. He'd brought me some daffodils, bought from one of those street vendors one sees every ten yards, in the springtime; the bunch just fitted into my big purse, a square sort of vanity case, portable closet and bathroom:

"I'll put them in some warm water as soon as I get home," I said. "That'll revive them right away, you'll see."

"I won't see.... Oh forgive me, Anne, I absolutely can't stay with you this evening."

When he explains to me about the friends he has to see a night, as he hastily leaves me, with a smiling tenderness for a good-bye, I cry a little inside, of course; but soon I accept the situation, I regain my composure.... The day before yesterday it was different: I sensed that Julien was going to stay in Paris, that he was leaving me to be with the other woman.... The other woman, whose presence and outlines become clearer and clearer, although Julien shrouds her in silence and mystery. Some day, I'm going to go after that shadow, I'll tear it apart ... no, it's I who is the shadow, my shadowy hands can't strangle even the neck of another shadow with enough force; I have to accept Julien with all his gang, and little by little get closer while saying "Excuse me," until I've joined him and am walking beside him, letting those people follow us or drop us, as they please; but first, get closer ...

I'd slammed the car door and I'd walked, as fast as my foot would let me, without turning around, without listening to the motor already fading into the din of the night traffic. In the métro, I watched myself crying in the window, Nation-Étoile, Étoile-Nation, "riding the métro," an old gimmick to get myself to sleep.

I got out one stop before my hotel: I wanted to get back to my bed on foot, and, if possible, find some bars still open on the way, where they wouldn't know me: the one in the hotel was incompatible with my thirst without limits, without elegance, my thirst without thirst. I drank several double cognacs one right after the other, and had a last one at the hotel—the others were still too recent to have taken effect: I felt absolutely nothing, neither dizziness nor warmth, I was cold and clear. I got my key, went up without using the elevator: I was putting off the moment when I would no longer be able to stand up, speak, walk. Already, thoughts were clearing out of my head, squeezing into a little corner, leaving only one fixed image: the bottle of Sherry Julien brought recently, not yet opened—I don't like it—on a shelf in the closet; the bottle

I was going to drink, fast, on which I was going to pounce before even starting to get undressed: to get up to the shelf I'd have to climb up on a chair, and the cognac was pounding now behind my eyes and ears. I then washed, in slow motion, taking a swallow between each gesture, listening to the alcohol take hold of my arteries and dissolve them; I poured the rest of the bottle into my toothbrush glass, I placed it within arm's reach and I fell onto the bed, exhausted.

For a day and a half, I hovered between life and death, rolled up in a sea of tangled blankets and sheets, which stifled me, bound me, then unknotted into anguishing and empty laces where I rowed and thrashed like a shipwrecked person. The telephone would ring, I would shout "Hello, hello," without thinking to pick it up; I watched for my death in the shadow of the curtains which remained closed, in the succession of dimness and absolute darkness.

Day, night, day: this morning I decided to start to live again, fearing that the chambermaids would end up opening my door with a passkey.

Tonight, I feel extraordinarily well. There's a fuzzy sensation behind my eyeballs; at times the voices, the sounds of the jukebox roar into a cataclysm, faces and objects balloon and explode before my eyes; then, I blink and everything resumes its normal aspect, clear-cut, reassuring.

"Oh, excuse me, Suzy...."

The guy who just came into the bar is one I've already "gone up with": I go up with them, sometimes I come back down with them, but I rarely go up with them again; tired of looking for me in places I say I hang around in, they find someone else or go away. But this one is particularly tenacious:

"I've been looking for you for a week," he says, sitting down in the place that Suzy, good buddy, had immediately freed, "the customer is sacred." "I've got a headache from swilling down pastis in all these bars. But I've found you again, that's the main thing."

He has thick, still-black eyebrows; his gray hair looks affected, artificial, bristly and crew-cut, above the face of a very young old man, chiseled, with limpid eyes, strong white teeth. I usually deflect men's kisses onto my cheek, but I almost feel like really kissing this one, who has restful lips, at once humble and voracious.... We come out of the hotel, we separate; then, at the same instant, we turn around, we come back to one another and we start walking side by side, in step with each other:

"Would you like to have dinner with me?"

I hesitate: I haven't filled my quota. I only have myself to account to, but I'm a rigorous self-employed woman.

"I'd love to ... but would you mind coming by to get me in an hour, or an hour and a half?"

"You have to work some more, is that it? Come for dinner: you tell me what I'll have made you lose, I'll give it to you...."

Funny, this guy: his clothes and his way of speaking run lower class, and yet he seems to have dough, manners, he's self-assured and courteous; for me he's like a place where one would sleep well, he is a brown shoulder where I could rest, my eyes full of the blond shoulder, oh, Julien ...

Taxi, Pigalle, restaurant, the check please, where do we go now? The movies, a night club, dancing, a show?

I don't want to be seen with this old man. I'll make him pay me and make me come, steal whatever he has and get away before dawn. He can't believe his ears: I'm free, really? I say:

"I don't have anyone in particular. Well, I ..."

No, I won't say anything.

"... at least, I don't live with him."

Tonight, it's really tough; the landladies are two old maids who are intransigent about nocturnal visitors; the guy goes up the stairs with catlike tread and I follow him, my shoes in my hand:

"By the way," he says, "you're the first one who's ever been up here."

"I can see why," I say, flinging my shoes across the room and stretching out my tired and swollen ankle on the nice smooth bedspread.

"Furnished apartments ..." I'd raised my eyebrows: what with the looks of the guy, I'd been planning on a rooming house rather than a luxurious apartment and I'd prepared myself for a polite silence; but suddenly I feel exhausted, exhausted to the point of no longer being able to move, make small talk, or put on any pretenses whatsoever. I let a drink be poured for me, the guy holds it up to my lips, I swallow it down like a baby, my tongue is burning, dirty, sour. He undresses me, slides the sheet under me and takes up a position, sitting on the edge of the bed. He's going to watch over me, and then what?

"Well, aren't you coming to bed too?"

Now, he's just a man, naked, anonymous, neither more nor less dreary than the others this afternoon, but who has the advantage over them of having a bed. After a while, I say:

"All right, that's fine like that...."

The poor thing, he wanted to give me some pleasure!

He makes a date for the following Sunday. I'd hoped to spend that weekend with Julien: my brush with death deserved some compensation, to my mind. But Julien hadn't telephoned.

Having nothing better to do, needing the money, I agree to go and spend the time with Jean, to eat and sleep with him; I also accept the contents of his wallet. He tells me the story of his life: he's a workman all right, but a specialist, an expert, who works on race cars with delicate entrails, during their lay-overs in the shop or behind scenes at the race tracks; Jean, who talks about engines like lovers, Jean, the mechanic.

When the people are too thick skinned, like those at Pierre's, for example, I don't try to be interesting: after a few unsuccessful or misinterpreted advances, I sink into the in-difference where they themselves have put me. Not out of contempt, but because I don't know how to open up people's ears or their hearts: they have to come to me. I go along with them, indifferent to their disdain, confident in their solicitude, smiling in their gaiety.

Jean bucks me up, comforts me, makes my legs appear to be alike:

"And you think you don't have pretty legs? But look at them, look at them in the mirror!"

All right: the right one looks like a pinup girl and the left one some kind of doll, why can't I believe him?

"Oh, Jean, stop kidding me, it makes me nervous."

In my mailbox, behind the desk, I find nothing, every night; every morning I wait for the telephone to ring, but he never calls me, that stupid instrument, that goddamned Julien, this goddamned life, goddamned life that I bless anyhow, every dawn when I open my eyes on the décor of my room, chosen above the cell they thought they would wall me up in.

"I'm doing all right, Julien...."

My savings are growing, I don't accumulate anything but money, I calculate: soon, I'll have enough to buy four walls of my own, I.... But I have to wait in this hotel room sitting by the phone, until Julien comes back and saves me again.

I won't force his hand anymore, I don't want him to weep in front of me anymore....

"Are you crying, Jean?"

"No, I just have a little cold...."

I'd been particularly horrible this evening: I'd refused to suck around at the table of the traitor, I'd found the sheets dirty and the tap water rather cool.... Lying down, six inches between us, we avoid each other: Jean flees from my words and I flee from his hands. He loves me and that bothers me, since I only love his bed. But the more I yell at him, the more he effaces himself, the more he melts into sweetness and light.... Then I feel guilty, to boost my spirits I drain the bottle which, since I got here, has been permanently enthroned on the religiously dusted and tidied bedside table, so I decide to be sweet. With my eyes closed, I accept Jean, I recognize his gentleness and his knowledge, I imagine the happiness he should be giving me and which I don't get, my face tight with grief, Julien, Julien ...

12

"Don't ever try to come to my mother's, don't leave Paris, wait for me, I'll always come back": too bad, I'm going to forget those wise words and go and find out. I'll prowl around the house, without letting myself be seen, and if Julien is there I'll be perfectly able to sniff out his presence. I have the telephone number he left me at the station: I'll look up the corresponding address and I'll go there. Even if I really put my foot in it: there is something wrong, this silence screams at me, I have to find out.

I take the train, empty-handed, hardly anything in my pockets: just my ticket and a little money. Tonight, I'll be back, with or without Julien, but in any case with some news of him.

I lean back against the plush headrest, looking out the window at the flat, sad countryside, the steady and fluid parade of telephone poles. Cine returns to sit beside me: the trip is the same, but this morning rain doesn't lash at good-byes to Paris, the sun is caressing, promising, free, Cine is dead and Julien is alive.

Here is the city: infallibly, I find my way through it, I get to the mother's house. It's ten-thirty, a good time, the kids are at school, Eddie at work, and I won't appear to be asking myself for lunch. I push open the garden gate, I'll go press my nose against the window in the kitchen door: I can see myself again, bloody and trembling, on the chair in front of the oven; miserable, gorged with chicken and sleep, at the Easter dinner; up there too, I am at the bedroom window: here is my longest, my best house.

"Madame!..."

The mother just came out, the salad basket in her hand; she's about to sprinkle the doorstep. Seeing me, she stops in mid-gesture, stunned, then her smile opens along with her arms; and instantly, our love for the same man creates a signal of understanding and anguish from her to me: Julien, my man, her son. Julien is between us and holds our hands together.

"Forgive me for having come, it's very risky, I know.... But I'm dying of worry: where is he?"

And the mother starts crying, huge silent tears: she is very tiny, just smaller than I am, and since age stoops her a little I have no trouble putting my arms around her. She carried Julien in her belly, Julien is still a part of her and, in the sense that he is my man and my brother, so his mother is my mother, my sister.

"What's the trouble, Mo ... Madame?"

"Julien wrote, day before yesterday: he's at X ... arrested, again.... He didn't give many details: the censorship.... Ginette went to see the magistrate to get a permit, I'll go and see him Saturday: they're almost always on Saturday, the visiting hours.... I don't even know if you can still see him every day, or if his case has been tried yet, nothing."

"But ... when did this happen?"

"Two weeks ago, I'm sure: he hasn't been here for the last two Sundays, and he always comes on Sunday, even it it's just for five minutes. When he can ..."

("Outside, you can do lots of things....")

I'm made to sit down, have lunch. The kids chatter away, all happy to see this lady whom they remember vaguely, but who they didn't think had any legs, or a bag, with candies inside it. Beneath their laughter, lies the weight of our concern. I am close to the mother, our love has the same quality; but Ginette.... "The old boy's in jail again, we'll have to take up our old habits, trotting to the post office window for money orders and to the visiting days, what will people think?" Ginette doesn't say anything, but I can read her thoughts....

Awkwardly, I try to offer some money; they tell me:

"Don't bother, he's got plenty of help."

The mother's pension, the brother-in-law's pay, are not enough to explain the "plenty"; and besides, there's someone other than the family and me in this room, someone who steals in and imposes himself, the shadow passes.... Why this reticence? They must know that I'm Julien's mistress, no? That they might dissuade me from writing him would be normal: even if he was still only detained, we don't know for what, and my scribbles couldn't possibly influence the magistrate, while if he's condemned, he would only be allowed to receive letters from his family anyhow. But a money order? A single, straightforward token, so as to intrigue the censors' only once, a token in memory of my foot, my foot of gold?

Obviously, I could leave them money which they could send: under their name: that would be "discreet and delicate." ... But I am neither discreet nor delicate, I have a lover's pride, and to send Julien money under another name doesn't interest me: for all the pennies Julien coughed up so that I could walk, I only want to answer with my own, if it's at all possible to reply to compassionate love with a few cents. ("You don't owe me a thing, little funny face! On the contrary, I'm in debt to you." Yes, Julien.)

On the train back to Paris, I think hard: with the warrant out against me, the risk is always the same, whether I hustle, whether I steal, whether I simply window-shop; no matter what direction I take, no matter what I do, I am in the wrong. Because I am there, instead of being in jail.

Jail is my right road.

Julien has gone back there in my place: I slip into his coat of pain and, beneath that armor, I follow my path and his; we are going one toward the other by strange routes....

I don't know how to work like he does, but I ask him to lend me the strength and the skill he left behind, useless, in the coatroom: infuse me with what I lack, Julien, protect me. As before, when the night didn't bring you back and I watched out for you, my head and my heart full of alarms, so I will watch out for my own return. And everything that I know about men, I will use against them.

The business with men bores me to death, but sometimes my attention latches onto shreds of information, highlights and defines them. So, I'd jotted in my address book the telephone number of an interesting guy: he's an accountant, handles lots of dough, not only counting and wrapping it in bundles, but also carrying it back and forth, between the bank and the office. These packages of bills mean no more to him than a brick to a mason: he's satisfied to get a little part of one at the end of the month, enough to live on and to sample, from time to time, a moment with girls like me.

I planned to send his receipts to Julien, I'd dreamed of wild schemes, holdups, operation-surprise: always that *Série Noire*.... But if I replace day with night, a gun with a key.... I quietly enter the deserted offices, I sneak through the vestibule, I visit the museum of hooded typewriters and silent filing cabinets.... Good Lord, I swipe the twenty or thirty thousand from the depths of the cashier's office and I can never go back there again. Oh well, let's give it a try anyhow:

"I feel like seeing you...."

It seems that I have a much more fetching voice over the phone.

"That would be fine.... No, not Saturday, I'm saying that that would be fine, but wait till I can find a time...."

Not to seem too eager, pretend to give him preference over a lot of other dates:

"I could get free tonight, if it's convenient for you?"

It's Sunday, the terrace and the street laze along. I am attentive, professionally solicitous and sweet; I've made myself up like a little girl, as he talks I examine a torn fingernail, I have no other worries:

"Honey, you seem tired, tonight? But I called you today, on purpose, so that you wouldn't come with your daily receipts and your just-got-out-of-work look. What's the matter?"

"I'm fine, I'm fine," the guy says, "only, my Sunday!... I spent the whole day working. Yes, at the end of the month, there's a terrible amount of accounting! Anyhow, it's all right, I finished it. I was planning to sleep in the office tonight, because of all the cash; but after all, I can be there first thing tomorrow morning and get back from the bank before the boss arrives.... Would you like to come to my place, or would you rather go to a hotel?"

In the middle of the night, I make sure the guy's sound asleep, and I sneak out of the house, the key to the office in my pocket. I leave my purse behind as a hostage, in case he wakes up too soon: Just a little errand I forgot, darling.

The time it takes to find a taxi to leave me off near the office, to climb the stairs four at a time after the automatic buzzer let me in without having to wake the concierge, I insert the minuscule key, the redoubtable key of the police lock, I push, I turn.... Whew, one or two hours ahead on breaking in.

Not one of the drawers is locked. In the accounting department I rifle the "petty cash," a few thousand, and get on with the search. The little shit, he's put the money in a piece of brown paper secured by a rubber band, at the very bottom of a drawer full of old folders. I tear open a corner, the bills appear, crisp and clean, brand new money.... I don't unwrap them, I stick the package down the front of my dress and stand up, a little dizzy. It's not possible that it was that easy, something's going to happen to me ... no, the offices continue to sleep, nothing moves in the building or in the street. The most delicate thing remains to be done: to make it look like a burglary, to cover the guy as well as myself.

Behind the boss's office, I discover a little cubbyhole, a sort of dressing room, with a sink and some clothes hooks, whose window gives onto a narrow street and consists of a pane of opaque glass. The window is locked. I open it, the night comes in to me, I breathe the enormous silence where only my heart beats, under the warm padding of the money. Under the sink, there is a bucket and a cloth: I wrap my left hand in the cloth, I press it against the window, I listen again ... with a sharp rap from the shoe I hold in my right hand, I hit the middle of the pane: it shatters, almost soundlessly. One by one I remove the fragments of glass, I place them carefully in the sink, on the towel rack; I scratch the walls, inside and out, to make traces of a climb and descent; I scatter pieces of glass under the window, and I hang the cloth back up again after having shaken it out.

I relock the door and leave. At top speed, I go back over the route I'd just taken a short while ago, the door of the house opens when I push it, good: my lover has slept soundly. He sleeps, dreaming of additions. I put the key back in his pocket, I hide the dough in my bag: with his natural discretion it would never occur to him to rummage in it while I was asleep, for ... I'm dead tired, the excitement has drained me, I have to sleep, sleep.... No, the alarm clock's going to ring, watch out, I must stay awake until morning. I slide into the bed and resume the night where I'd left it. Let's be a whore, let's say: "Darling..." The guy presses me against his skinny chest, with his whole hairy body tensed and his nose trembling he tells me that he loves me, that I'm not like the other little girls, that the sidewalk doesn't become me and he's willing to do anything to get me off it:

"You could live here, I'm all alone. You could do as you pleased, even hustle if you wanted, but ... why keep on with that awful profession? I'd give you whatever you wanted...."

"But what about my boyfriend, did you forget about him? And would you like to be arrested as a pimp, if the cops find out that I'm living with you? No, darling, it's out of the question: you just don't understand the rules of the game...."

"But I love you...."

Yesterday Jean, now this jerk! How boring they are with their "I love you," how far away they are from love!

I smile at the thought that I'm sticking this guy by hiding

money stolen from his office right in his own apartment, and I wonder how on earth he'd get off in case of an impromptu search: complicity, harboring a criminal, plus.... Plus unnatural practices, if I decide to tell the whole truth about the habits of an accountant, even an expert and apparently chaste.

But now, how to unload this loot?

It bulges in my purse, like a perilous hernia; I can spend it and spend it and not earn a thing, the lump still doesn't diminish quickly enough. I have the feeling that people are staring at it, looking at my lump with the eyes of a cop, as they used to have the eyes of an expert on pretty legs, when I first limped out with my mismatched ankles.

I can't leave the thing at the hotel, where everything that locks can be opened in my absence; or at the bank, or in a checkroom like in my *Série Noire*; and who would love me enough, here, in this world, to prefer me to a pile of dough, stolen once, stolen twice, what would it matter?

I look at Annie, with her clear, slow eyes, her eyes of a whore who calls herself an orphan, her eyes of a mother and a friend.... For a while now, I've been making it be Christmas in May at her place: I brought Nounouche a mechanical horse, her favorite "outsider" of the horses in the Luxembourg Gardens, the only ones I could treat her to before.... And Nounouche, with the fickle heart of a kid, has forgotten that before she used to treat me like one of her little playmates and clawed at my heart with her childish cruelty, without my being able to answer back, spank her, or explain to her. Now, she is almost too polite. When I take her out, she walks beside me, her good little hand in my hand, she doesn't break away anymore to cross the street and doesn't question any of my tastes: fine about that perfume for her mother, yes, she likes to play Monopoly, "Get whatever kind of cookie you want, Anne, I like them all."

Annie is truly astounded: it's not possible that I could earn so much just with my little ass, and Julien can't have anything to do with it, since.... But in our world, as she says, whether you're on the lam or whether you're out hustling, gold is worth nothing compared to silence; and my silence, silly and joking as it may be, makes me very valuable. Well then, let's take a deep breath:

"Annie, would you mind keeping a package for me for a couple of days? I want to take a vacation, and I don't want to have to lug it around with me. I'd rather leave without any bags, or any destination, just to make the time pass a little quicker, until Julien gets out.... He's in jail, I'm going to get away: the sea, the sun, sleep ..."

"But Anne, this is your home, here. Leave anything you want with me. Even, perhaps you might like to come back and live here until Julien's out?"

So that's how it is: but when he got back I'd be as naked as when he left. No. Annie puts the package into a suitcase, on top of the closet, where mine sat for such a long time: the loot is stuck in between letters from Dédé and other bundles of precious papers, bills, souvenirs, all sorts of yellowing things.

"There, see, nobody can get at it. I keep this suitcase locked."

And Annie suggests having duplicate keys made for the suitcase and the door locks, so I could have access to my treasure even if she were away; she is my buddy, everything, lovingly, ingeniously, anxiously.

Her concern is all I have in the world.

13

I pay my hotel bill, I take my bags over to Jean's:

"You see, I accept ... here are my clothes already, the rest will follow."

I've placed my dough, my clothes and myself in separate drops; useless to wonder now what would have happened with the clothes at Annie's, the dough at Jean's, or me at Jean's with the whole works, or me alone with it all: what's done is done, I'm taking off for a few days to think about nothing, I'm taking the *train bleu*, I.... But I endlessly toss and turn, I go back and beat myself against the place where my heart is locked up: look, Julien, look at the gray sea showing through the dawn and feel bow cold I am, even though I'll soon be swimming.

Last night, the train was jumping with noisy, starving, excited people; the keyed-up bunches of children mingled with the laughing and scolding bunches of adults, the burdened mothers, the dire warnings. I'd found a seat between a detective-story reader and a teenager, also reading, but whose eyes kept sliding over to me. This morning the teenager is standing beside me in the corridor, and our sweetly held hands make a frail bridge between his unknown and my solitude:

"If you like," he says, "could we go swimming as soon as we get there? The water's nice, in the morning. I'll stop by my parents', get my suit and meet you somewhere: what do you say?"

The kid is healthy, tanned, bracing as a vacation drink; I feel old and broken down, I envy his youth:

"No; I'm going to find some sort of hotel, come with me, and come back and get me this afternoon. Do you know a good hotel, not too expensive but not too crummy?"

I've had my fill of glittering, formal hotels. I'd like to forgo an elevator, climb up stairs that weren't perfectly regular, with fresh red bricks, whitewashed crevices, acutely-angled landings; the sheets would be rough and lavender-scented, the window would not open onto the street: at night, the smell of garlic and onions would come up to me, with the murmur of the interior courtyard and the muffled breathing of the sea. It would be the Provence of postcards, with those same colors which take on reality and luster as we walk, the teenager and I, in that slow way, leading from the hips, peculiar to people on the coast, in summer.

My room is just as I hoped it would be: I spend an hour or two in it. The closed shutters let a golden pathway filter in where, like minuscule grains of sand, insects and dust float.

I've played with the boy; our bodies purr, emptied and supple. In a while, perhaps, we'll be hungry and thirsty again, we'll go down to the paneled dimness of the bar, or else we'll go and lie on the beach again. We'll say see you tomorrow, and tomorrow, I will have disappeared into another crowd of swimmers, alone or with someone else, but always isolated in my own circle or my own rectangle, with the innocent and merciful beauty of the water and the pine trees; step by step, I go toward my summer. I will arrive prepared, I neither attach nor define myself, to be able to model myself to the form my love will have by then.

Again I walk, my feet are yellow with dust, and the people around me envelop me, carry me, jostle me without bothering me, like waves; I walk, passive, neither happy nor sad. The warmth of the sun stores itself up in me, not yet radiating out: soon I'll be going back up into the cold again, I'll need my supply.

With my foot, I can no longer walk without shoes: the sole of my foot is hard and calloused, but it's gotten sensitive as the tenderest membrane, the least little pebble pierces it with pain. My leg no longer is the sure half-base of my equilibrium, each step is a pretense, a rectified fall; if I stop thinking about my walk, I immediately find myself limping and putting my foot down crookedly, at the angle learned in the "slightly equine" cast, as the records put it.

Walk straight, Anne: if you're recognized, if you're questioned, that accident must never come to light, your foot could mean prison for those who saved it. But ... how can I think about prison, here? How even believe in it? Here, everyone seems disguised, and the ever-present police ignore the crowd that I resemble, with my straw hat and my dark glasses.

At eight o'clock, I go down to the beach, and I stay there until evening, only leaving my rectangle of towel to go and take a dip: I swim a little, not very far, and I come back and throw myself down under the sun, flat on my back or flat on my stomach. Around seven, when the water gets cooler and the boys start their rounds, looking for a dancing or dinner date, I leave. I take a shower to wash off the salt, I get dressed and go up into town, a little beat, gorged with the odor and the rippling of the sea. In town, I do my shopping. I never liked sitting alone in a restaurant: here, as in Paris, I buy things wrapped in paper and eat them in bed, with a Kleenex for a tablecloth, while reading; raw things, things to be cooked that I don't cook, hamburger covered with pepper, and pounds of fruit, washed down with instant coffee. When Julien comes back to me, if ever we live and eat together, I'll fall back on my course in Household Management, I'll make civilized meals, decorated, simmered; but Julien is in jail, I'm on the run and happiness is very far away.

From Nice, I telephone Jean:

"Come and meet me at the train, I'm getting in tomorrow morning."

Bound by that rendezvous, I'm naturally obliged to get a ticket; otherwise, I could easily stay here until fall, stretched out, lazy.... Shake yourself, girl, you're black enough, your teeth have whitened in your smile, and when they approach you people will ask: "Do you speak French?" Julien won't find the pale child of that first night, I will be a Negro and beautiful and I will please him like a new woman. Even the scar on my foot which has gotten tanned.... My asymmetry? Pff, I am a charming mulatto who limps a little, that's all. No one will see the white triangles left by my bikini, no one will know that I come from the shadows and am going back into them.

Jean, who has made trips to Madagascar, calls me "my little *Antandrouille*," the whores cheer me: "Oh that beautiful black girl!" and I, to keep my tan going, take the métro every morning from Lilas to the Tourelles swimming pool. Until noon, I watch the professional divers practice, the crawl champions endlessly doing their lengths, I take a few strokes myself.... Here, too, the boys circle around my tan, pale boys for whom I invent a mother who's a good cook, and who doesn't stint on the slaps if you're too late getting to the table. I also have a profession, I start work at two: excuse me, I have to leave now.

The other day, coming out of Suzy's bar at an hour when I was supposed to be dutifully typing, I found myself face to face with the swimming instructor.... I pay attention to every face, to the expression I put on mine, at every step I take in Paris; but the guy has only seen me in a bathing suit and mustn't have recognized me. I nevertheless spent the evening making up a plausible excuse for the next day; but I didn't need it, neither the swimming instructor nor I made the slightest allusion to our little run-in in the red light district, and we spent the morning gently kidding each other, as usual. I said to him:

"Soon, you won't be seeing me here anymore...."

"Oh, what a shame! Are you leaving Paris?"

Yes: it's a month since I went to see the mother, Julien must have been sentenced by now. I have to go back, to find out when he'll be getting out. The protective edge is blunting, the supply of sun diminishes, I'll go and recharge myself.

But first, recharge my pocketbook at Annie's.

Annie's confusion is too obvious: the phrases she stammers out in a well-ordered jumble must have been rehearsed in front of the mirror. Out of her horse mouth, the words run like the knots in a line: unmoved, I wind in the line, tugging it gently when the reel gets stuck. I feel neither surprise, nor frenzy, just a little sadness with a vague desire to vomit that gathers under my ribs. I smoke and I breathe, regularly, air, smoke, air, smoke, I smoke my cigarette, I cling to it.

Nounouche is immobilized in front of the buffet, one foot

on top of the other; she's waiting for the go-ahead signal of my smile to throw herself on me, on Anne rediscovered under the black skin, clamber up my chair and rummage in my purse; but I do not smile at her. Nounouche is Annie's daughter, a promise of Annie, her eyes deep-set and full of images are already those of her mother. It's to Annie that my gaiety goes, for the death of an adult friendship is much less serious than the death of Nounouche.

When I feel the reel half-full, I ask:

"But how could anyone have gotten in? You're always home at night, and during the day the stairs are full of people."

"Well ... I think it happened while we were at the movies. Nowadays, without you, the evenings seem long, you know.... And it's so nice out, at night! Nounouche doesn't want to sleep without me, she's afraid that I won't come back, that I'll be taken to the hospital like her father ... so, I bring her along. Mostly on Saturdays, so that she can sleep late the next day: this year, she has to go to school, isn't that right?"

"Listen, Mama ..."

I put the conversation back on the tracks and, finally, Annie begins coughing up several knots at a time and choking herself. To compensate, she forces out a few tears, which ruin her mascara and increases my desire to laugh. I get up, I go and open the door, I test the bolts and the key, still in the lock as always, on the inside: the bolts are intact, of course. On the other hand, the central lock—a small one without force or complexity—shows signs of having been tampered with. Annie's words that last night, and all the others when she went to bed first, echoed in my ear: "Above all, don't forget to bolt the door...." We used to turn the key too, sometimes, mechanically: the door, without the bolts, didn't seem safe to us. I straighten up and say:

"This lock has never been forced, now come on! Those file marks, or whatever they are, that's a lot of horseshit, a bad movie! Well Annie, put it in a Western, you were out of your head, that night."

It's Annie's turn to bend over and study the damage to the door; this lasts a moment, then she turns a completely bewildered face to me: she can't pull that one off either, but then, if they got in with the keys.... She thinks hard, reviews all the people, over the years, that she and Dédé had lent their keys to and who (admitting that at the time they might have thought of having duplicates made) would now take advantage of the fact that she's living alone, to.... Poor Annie, she just doesn't have a gift for improvisation. I'm miffed that she could have thought for a second that I would swallow such a pile of crap; but she's trying so hard to clear out the debris, that I end up taking part:

"All right, let's not discuss it anymore...."

Annie's eyes lighten several shades.

"... Give me back what there is left and let's forget that there ever was any more. Because I don't think you could have blown it all, could you?"

The way I've seen Annie behave in the last hour, she wouldn't have had the nerve to take the whole thing: even when she does her dirty work, she bungles the job. Half-remorse or half-panic, in either case the thing is half-done. What a waste! For a couple of hundred francs, you screw up the millions in the future, you screw up yourself....

Annie rummages in the bedroom closet, comes back with a package wrapped in newspaper which she throws onto the table, she drops into her chair at the same time that the package drops between us:

"I've been terribly upset about this whole thing," she says. "Look, I haven't even had the strength to put everything back in place, 'they' upset everything...."

Since the joint is always a mess, I hadn't noticed that it looked even worse: but it's true, today it looks ransacked rather than just accumulated....

"... Or even to count: anyhow, I didn't know exactly how much you'd left with me."

Annie scratches her head, sits up, and goes on, in her usual voice:

"You understand, after you left, I took the dough out of the suitcase and hid it somewhere else; I changed the place several times, I could never find one that was safe enough: you know how Nounouche is always climbing around and poking into everything. Finally, I divided it into several packages which I put in different places...."

"In other words, you thought that the sucker was about to return?"

"No, but I was anxious for you to get back, Anne, I assure you. I'd rather hide ten pimps on the lam than a friend's money."

"Ten pimps take up quite a lot of room, however...."

"Yes, but they don't attract robbers."

"They attract whores, that's not much better...."

"Oh them, I wouldn't let them in the door!... But actually, Anne, tell me how much is missing: as soon as Dédé gets out, I'll pay you back, on my word. After all," she concluded, regaining her experienced, maternal tone, "what's money? It's out there on the street corner, all you have to do is go and get it.... If you don't get there fast enough?... You still have this to tide you over, and besides Julien will be back soon, so don't worry."

I've finished adding up what's missing: I fold the rest of the bills and wrap them in the dog-eared newspaper. So, on the linoleum of the table, the linoleum of feasts and former confidences, my fortune seems without value, without mystery other than the threads of printed words surrounding it, the dirty fabric without significance: yesterday's newspaper, or last month's, stale words hiding crisp new money. The rest of it Annie will convert into goodies for Dédé or steak for Nounouche: the end justified the means. There's nothing left for me to do but get out:

"Well, see you later, Annie. And don't get all worked up over such a minor thing: as you say, Julien will be here soon. Dédé too, you'll see. They can take care of this much better than we can. You're my buddy, I can't argue accounts with my buddies...."

I go back to Jean's: Julien's house is too far away, the train is dreary, and I feel like sleeping, drinking, laughing.

However, I climb the stairs of the apartment house in tears, my heart and my feet equally bare, my shoes in my hand.

I had agreed to live with Jean because he said he was often away on business trips, all over France: over our first drinks, we had no subject of conversation except our activities, and Jean only talked about his trips; I could follow him by remembering things I had read and promised to go with him.... Unfortunately, ever since I got here, Jean never goes anywhere: he has himself replaced, on the pretext of illnesses and is, actually, very tired. Tonight, the minute I get in the door his presence depresses me; not so much he himself, sitting in an uncluttered corner, but the arrangement of his little décor, his meticulous neatness that has mixed my things up with his in a faultless order; even the pieces of uranium floating in glass globes, the sand roses and quartz brought back from Africa have lost, so carefully lined up, all radiation and all sparkle. My phonograph, whose cover serves as a storage space for records, is violated by a dust rag, all clean; my clothes and my shoes are packed in with Jean's in the closet which is topped off by a large bouquet of plastic roses. I spot several little packages sitting on the kitchen cupboard, some crisp—the cookies; others starting to get greasy and run—things from the delicatessen. At the sight of these preparations, Jean's questioning eyes, I burst into sobs, I walk over to him and I let myself be held in his arms, kissed, have my hair stroked.

Jean's shirt smells of the laundry, soapy sweat; he keeps caressing my head, mechanical and applied, repeating:

"But what is the matter? What happened to you, tell me? I never saw you cry!..."

"Well, you won't be able to say that anymore. I suppose it gives you a big kick, seeing me cry!"

"Of course not ... I'm here, I'll help you, tell me...."

I throw the dirty newspaper onto the sofa: the bills, pinned together in tens, slide to the floor like a deck of cards, triumph, Rolande.... Hey, this might be the moment: a few months late, except for my ankle, I am what I dreamed of being like for this meeting. Only, there is my ankle.

To have mutilated myself so horribly, to have been so miraculously saved and put back together, is a sign, the prelude and the condition of something, a thing much more important than an adulterated love born in jail and half-dead with neglect.

Jean's eyes bug out of his head: he can't often have seen so much loot spread out on the rug. I push the last bills so that they fall to the floor with the others, I put a record on the phonograph, I turn the volume up as high as it will go to irritate the neighbors and I say to Jean:

"Come and sit down! You're walking, pacing, circling. Is 'that' what excites you? *Peuh*, me, it makes me cry, come to think of it."

I arrange my feet on the bills, I let Jean begin stroking my head again, and I tell him, everything: what happened since my return from the coast, I go back to before the coast, before him, Julien, the broken foot, the escape, prison, the court. A long silence ensues, Jean's hand interrupts its stroking and lies, heavy, on my shoulder. I go on:

"You know, you only have to say the word, and I'll pack my suitcase: after all, I'm compromising you too.... Less than the others, of course: you are ... you are my client, and, as far as the landlord knows, I don't exist. But how could you say that I don't live here? There are the things in the closet, my picture ..."

I lean back to snatch from the bedside table the photo which shows me, in a bathing suit, on the beach: a picture taken by a roving photographer which I sent Jean from Nice, to tide him over till I got back:

"Aren't you nuts to keep this? I'm a fugitive, do you realize what that means?"

"But baby," Jean says, "I've only known that for five minutes.... Wait a minute, let me digest all this.... You're exhausting, did you know that?"

And his hand resumes its caress, this time on my arm. When Jean speaks again, his voice is unfamiliar, precise, hard:

"Nothing is changed. You stay here and, if the cops get mixed up in it, I'll know what to tell them: I have nothing to hide, and you ... you, I won't hide you either. You've done enough tiptoeing up in your bare feet, tomorrow I'll find a place where we can both register. What could they possibly do to me? Your papers are in order, didn't you say?"

"Yes, forged, but to register, they'd be all right."

"Good. Anyhow, we'll think up a good story. And while I'm doing that, you go to your man's house and find out how he's doing. No but Anne, perhaps he's already out, he's looking for you in Paris, what if that's the case?"

I think: the joint is bearable, Jean isn't throwing me out, why not stay here? Obviously, I'd have to pay, keep my words and my body lovable.... Heck, I'll just drink a little more. But Jean goes on:

"Of course, I would never ask anything more of you: a *ménage à trois*, no, not for me. And your man might not agree to it either. You come here, you eat, you sleep, you do as you like. As for me, well, you see, Anne, if you feel like coming back here from time to time, even just to stop by for five minutes, I'd be very pleased. Because I would see you, I would know that you were happy.... Now, does that suit you?"

"Listen, Julien isn't here yet, and I'm not his wife. I could say no, to him, to you, to everyone. Since my escape, I've been nothing but 'the package,' and now, for you too! You want to carry me! Oh, Jean, I would like to go away, go back to the sea, be alone, alone, die...."

I start to sob. Jean waits until I've finished, then he suggests that we go out, I need a change, that business with Annie has gotten me down, but:

"Come on, let's go out, we'll go wherever you want.... What do you say, Anne? ... And stop crying, you can't imagine what it does to me."

"No, we'll set out the little packages, and then go to sleep."

A part of me sleeps with Jean, wakes up to Jean's alarm clock, meets Jean in the evening. Sometimes I call him at work to say I'll come and pick him up, and to get there I take murderous subway rides: it takes longer than a cab. To draw out the time even further, I linger with Jean on the boulevards warm with people and sun, I let him take me into shops, or into parts of Paris that he shows me and tells me about: his Paris, that he offers me. Then, like two happily married people, we go to the market, the bakery shop, the delicatessen, always: I hardly ever touch the stove, the way Jean has of being enraptured and overjoyed at the slightest thing I cook is indigestible.

We've moved: the room is much less splendid than the other one, but I have official access to it, they skimmed through my papers at the desk and they call me Madame Jean's-Last-Name. The courtyard is full of kids, the windows full of laundry, and there is no running water; but this worker's life, on the whole, pleases me.

My bathroom is at the end of the hall, in the toilets: my feet on the footrests of the Turkish toilet, I pour basins of cool water on my shoulders, I hold my legs under the faucet set in the opposite wall, at knee height. When I come out, wrapped in a towel, the neighbors are gathered on the landing, their receptacles in their hands, for that faucet is the only one on the floor. But nobody minds: it's the landlord who complains.... I don't care: my shower kills a half an hour, I keep on taking them twice a day.

The rest of the day, I read Jean's books, I leaf through his files, technical, touristic, private; I smile out of the window at the little faces in the courtyard, I wait for my husband to come home. Nobody seems astonished at my youth compared to Jean's gray hair, at our hand-in-hand of lovers: I drop Jean's hand once we've crossed the threshold of the building, he crooks his arm, I take it: that's how you have to do it. In that place, it's normal to live with someone much older or younger than yourself, to gossip, to drink, to fight. The exotic note is lent by two roomfuls of blacks, their black wives and children: they don't shout, they sing, and the spicy odor of their cooking seeps in under the doors. Which inspires Jean to tell me again about his colonies, while I listen to my transistor radio with the other ear, taking a drink from time to time out of the bottle of cognac on the floor. He never says anything, Jean, about my drinking, about my going out on the town ("Taking a walk? Mind if I come along?"), about my coming home too tired to feel like responding to him.... My purse open on the bed, I count the bills earned during the afternoon.

"But really," Jean says, "I don't understand you: since you have money anyhow, why go out and risk getting caught? especially since you don't even like them, those types!"

"But Jean, do you think I love you? And anyhow, I come back here every evening, or almost. Why? Because it suits me, do you understand, because it suits me. But I don't give a damn about you, about them, about the whole world. But I do keep the money, because it doesn't belong to me, it's Julien's too, and we'll go through it together. I want to keep it all for him, intact, with the little bit of love I am capable of...."

Jean takes this very well, I even think he likes it. I put him off, I make myself cold, I drink, I collapse, I sleep until Jean wakes me with coffee, bread that he has cut and buttered himself, without making any noise, so that I'll be in a good mood when I open my eyes; he is already ready to go to work, dressed, shaved, his briefcase in his hand. At those moments, I make myself very loving....

"So, Jean, what about the track?" I say afterwards.

"Well, I'll be late, so what?"

A soft nest for twenty-four hours: I could go out, in a while, and stay out all night if I want. But I always sleep out as little as possible: my foot gets hot, it thirsts for old slippers and fresh sheets, and I try to stop myself at the edges of any possibility of sacrilege; if a man has Julien's eyes, or if he carries his briefcase as Julien did, or if he speaks to me with his voice, I turn away and run to Jean, Jean who, at least, has nothing I am tempted to love: his body doesn't disgust me, he is friendly and unsurprising, docile, agreeable, that's all. It's his self-effacement that I detest, his resignation, his sympathetic smile in which little twinges of grief sometimes appear.

14

"You'll stay overnight, won't you? Your bed is still there...."

I'd been meaning to take the train back that same night, but Eddie insists, I suppose he has something to tell me in private. So I accept the invitation.

After dinner, Ginette goes up to put the kids to bed, the mother kisses me and retires to her room: I am alone with Eddie in the dining room. He puts a stack of records on the phonograph, sits down beside me and takes a tiny piece of yellowed paper out of his wallet:

"Here," he says, "it's a note from Julien, for you. Don't tell mother or Ginette: there's no point in worrying them."

I unfold it. Before the greeting, Julien had written: "Part of three notes." Another for the family, the third for the other woman, surely.... But the first words remove all doubt, and there, in front of Eddie who has sunk down into the sofa, closed his eyes and is drinking in his music with devotion, I read, my heart dying, my face transfixed with joy.

Julien begins by giving me a few hints about the nature of the affair and the conduct I should adopt during the trial: "Go and see the lawyer, he's an old ass, but *only go once*. Tell him that you're coming on your own initiative and that there's no point in my knowing about it.... He's been paid: don't give him any dough, but offer it to him," etc.

In brief, beneath this minor infraction of traveling privileges (Julien was caught coming here), I read his concern about being accused of several burglaries committed in the region: if that should be the case.... "The only way never to lose each other again is never to leave each other again: if I go convicted, I'll just do the time; however, with you, I'd almost rather break out...."

"But Eddie, where does he stand now? This note is dated before the trial: do you have anything more recent?"

Eddie hesitates:

"Yes ... that, those were the first ones we got, hidden in the first package of dirty laundry; we've gotten others since then, but ... for you, I only have that one. But you'll be seeing him soon: he's getting out on June 21st."

"And when was his trial?"

"Wait ... it must be hardly ten days ago, the courts were slow. The prosecutor grilled him a couple of times in jail; he started getting very bugged and wanted to get out of there ... finally everything worked out: they didn't find anything, at his place, in his car, or here."

"They came here?"

Eddie shrugs his shoulders:

"What do you think? As usual: a search, the mother and my wife interrogated.... This time, they went through the joint from eight o'clock in the morning till six at night, it was quite a scene when I got back from work! In the end, they didn't bother me too much."

In those cases, Eddie prefers being the father of Julien's nephews to being the husband of his woman. When he got out of Central, five years ago, Eddie had been taken in at Julien's and had appealed to Ginette: he had moved in for good and exchanged his skin for clean laundry and a pair of slippers; the children whom he took over, as he says, "readymade," call him Papa: this reciprocal adoption allows him to play the leading role and Eddie plays it skillfully.

I suddenly wonder what name my kid would have, if Julien knocked me up.... But I'm being an ass, I'd never have an il-legitimate child, that, no! I go on:

"Of course, you'll be going to get him, on the 21st? I'll come with you, I'd like to."

Eddie, whom nothing ever seems to bother, looks away; the silence deepens and lengthens.

"How about one last drink before going to bed?" Eddie sug-gests. "Listen, Julien wrote me about just that. Tell me where he can meet you, sometime after the 21st, and I'll give him the message. He'd rather you didn't take any chances around the prison, you never know: 'they' might be following him...."

"Well, I wouldn't be standing right in front of the door, I'm not that dumb!... But why not somewhere in town, some bar, I don't know!"

And suddenly, I feel excluded again, a beggar at the gate, facing into the group, facing into the shadows, I hurt.... I sit back up, I fish my date book out of my purse and I look through it for a mo-ment. Luckily, there are quite a few things written for between the 20th and the 25th of June: errands, people to see, telephone numbers and hours. I pretend to think, to take my time:

"O.K.; I'm free the 24th in the evening: can you remember that? It's easy, it's St. John's day.... Let's make it here...."

"No, no …"

"I mean, in town, at the bar across from the station, for example, at … let's say seven?"

I wasn't too difficult: relieved, Eddie resumes his mediating tone, quietly:

"Three days! But supposing Julien wants to see you sooner? How can he get hold of you?"

I'm not about to give him Jean's address.

"Well, he can wait. The Lord knows, I've waited! Don't forget: St. John's Day, Anne, seven o'clock."

We listen to a few more records, Eddie keeps calling me *tu*, then *vous*, we must both have been a little drunk.

… St. John's Day is tomorrow. I would like to empty my head, my guts, and my veins, endlessly wash and scrub my skin. I would like Julien to completely fill me, to use me and in return be available, whole.… I write one last note, after all those written in solitude, in the sun, in boredom: all the letters I never mailed, but saved in the certainty that some day, Julien would read them. In jail, one reads one's mail with an attention that is too intense, selective, deforming.

Julien in jail is not the Julien I know, nor the one that I will find; even if he persists in veiling himself in fog, this fog will have a different density. Maybe, like the girls in Central whom we would accompany to the cell for those who had served their term on the eve of their departure, he will have that strange expression, deprived, the face of someone who has lain down his arms because he finally has won.

Oh, I'm making too much out of a few months in the shadows!… After my years in Central, when Julien picked me up, I didn't look all that victorious.… And even now, I wonder if ever I will be able to lay down my arms.

Tomorrow, tomorrow.... As usual I am lying on the bed, with the sheet pulled up to my neck so that Jean doesn't feel like making me: saying nothing, I stare at the cracks in the ceiling. Jean comes and goes in the room, with heavy steps, he moves things, puts others away: viewed in silence and slow motion, it's a crisis for him and for me. I tell him to come and sit down on the bed and I read him parts of my letters.

"No doubt about it," he says, "you have style."

"Do you really think he'll like these things?"

"I'd love to have gotten them myself!"

I remember the value of mail, the intensity we put into getting it or waiting for it; but, in jail, your thoughts get confused, images buzz around like huge captive insects, you chase them, you catch them, you pin them down, and somehow you murder them: in letters, received or sent, you exaggerate, you omit, you distort.... And you would have wanted me to write you, Julien, at a time when your head was full of this sort of thing? The denials and resolutions forged in prison, sometimes it just takes one hour to dissolve them.... If I believe your words today, it's because I want to, need to. Tomorrow ...

"Are you going to take your suitcase?" Jean asks.

He's sure that I'm leaving forever; and, in fact, if I take all my things away, why come back? Nothing more ties me to this place: Jean just gave me back the rest of the money, which he'd been keeping for me in a special hiding place that he made me check from time to time. The money is in my purse, I could pack in a minute ... Jean would rejoice in my happiness, weeping of course, and not doing anything to hold onto me; it would be ghastly. On the other hand, I don't know at all what Julien's plans are but, ahead of time, I approve of all of them: we might be going very far away, but also we might be staying in Paris or nearby, and not necessarily living together, being on the run, the need to sleep and change the sheets ... I sit down on the bed:

"I'm leaving my things here," I say. "Would you mind taking my suit to the cleaners? Don't worry, Jean, I'll be back soon....

Julien, hang onto me, don't let me come back, keep me from doing what I don't want to do.... Perhaps we'll learn to become vigilant and jealous of one another, to react and cry like everyone else....

How slowly the clock moves! The sheet sticks to my chest, oppresses me a little. I would like to sleep, to become a mineral, to be a block around my heart which leaps and bounds ahead of me: choose it, Julien, the path that I am, jump onto it with both feet and let me forever support all of your footsteps.

... As I pour the water into the glass, slowly, the liquid rises and clouds. It's my paint water: I've amused myself by coloring the bar and the tables yellow; I leave the waiters' jackets and the girls' blouses white, the rest I drown in color: the immobile parade of bottles on the shelves, confusion of their labels, dark with writing and brown skins, light with summer clothing.

My head is spinning, I haven't had a drink for three days. I pick up my glass, then I put it down: for this particular glass I want to wait and toast to our finding each other again. The preceding ones have been drunk, eclipsed and washed down but this one is here to stay, intact, in the décor whose parts assemble themselves, bit by bit, as I sit here, watching the clock above the bar. Five to seven: in five minutes, I will stop the film. The people in the station, the trains going by, the whistles and vapors of the nearby track, everything is a screen around me, I who would like to pin down, like a film clip, the part that I would star in. The shadows dissolve tonight, and the sunshine floods me.... Three minutes before seven.

I won't look at that clock anymore, nor at the people going in and out of the door. Julien will come in one of those bursts of people, my eyes wait for him, lowered, blind; I collect my look, my hands and my feet, I gather myself together, and still the people pass by with the seconds, without attracting my attention: liquid running over smoothness, vagueness over softness.... I am *here*, it's true: I'm on the right track again after having limped and lingered in dark passages; but I was always heading here, guided and aimed in this particular direction. I never lost my compass, hello! Julien.

He looks at his watch:

"I think this is probably the first time that I've ever been on time...."

He'd slid into the booth beside me, before I'd really recognized him. I hastily try to connect, to locate the threads of reality, but my brain gets lost in my eyes, without being able to say anything to him I look at Julien: and all the questions, all the agonies and all the promises melt, disappear and fulfill themselves in that second when we look at each other.

Like a huge black and white insect, the waiter goes around, infallibly attracted by the tables where there's a glass missing: for him, my Ricard only accounts for me; Julien has to exist for the waiter too, the waiter who prowls around with a watchful indifference, manipulating his tray and his napkin, bumping into the empty chairs. He is insupportable.

"Waiter!" I ask Julien, quietly, what he'd like to drink, I add "Another Ricard," the waiter goes off, Julien begins to exist more and more.

I hardly recognize him: he is pale, a mustache has grown like a caressing accent on the flesh above his lips; his face is rested, as though purified, he scares me like a sacred or forbidden thing. It's he, Anne, that's your lover, but he's also just like any guy who gets out of prison in the morning, or passes in front of the barroom door: is it then so natural, so necessary, to love this one? The thing that passes and crackles from his body to mine, what is it, where does it come from?

We talk: words that explain ourselves, free us and accompany the profound silence of our impressions. I talk about myself and he talks about himself: we, that is the silence, that will come later. Three months plus three months, six months of separation, there's a lot to tell; the waiter has turned on the lights and refilled our glasses, but our hunger for words is not filled.

Julien tells me the details of his arrest, the interrogations of the judge, his fears for me:

"Like a jerk, I had your telephone number in my address book, and I had the address book on me, as usual. There was no way to get rid of it, I was wearing handcuffs and they were searching me.... How they bugged me about that number! I finally told the truth: that it was a hotel that had been recommended to me.... They jumped on that: "Oh! Then you must go to Paris?" I answered that I hadn't had the chance since they'd arrested me on the way.... You can imagine how worried I was, that they might question the desk clerk and go through the guest list...."

I laugh at that:

"But honey, once I got wind of things, do you think I stayed around there? They might have come at any time...."

(Now, for Jean:)

"So, before looking for a new pad, I decided to wait for you and leave my things with this guy. A nice guy, by the way, but that doesn't mean I have a place to live.... I'm hero as usual, you see: without a name, without anything, naked, or almost, like that first night.... Oh yes, wait: there's a little dough, I brought it for your, well really for our initial expenses."

I hold the brown paper package out to Julien, I try to make the gesture seem casual and natural: it's hard to give someone money, almost as hard as getting it. We know that too well not to always play a little game of reluctance. I remember how Julien used to do it, at Annie's: he'd shove it into my pocket or my hand saying "Here, get yourself a pair of stockings." No matter how large the amount was, it was always for a pair of stockings. So, I say:

"Here, it's for gas.... And since I'm coming with you, get a car too, a little bigger than the other one. By the way, where is the other one?"

"Eddie went and got it at the station: those rotten guys had put it in storage, I had to make out a slip, get permission from the presiding judge.... Anyhow, since Eddie carried the whole thing off all right and Ginette adores to be driven around, I told them to keep it: they can wear it out."

"We'll start on another one, a brand-new one...."

"Absolutely not! A car's a thing you buy secondhand, then it doesn't matter so much if you crack it up. I'll go back to Paris, to the guy who sold me the other one. Now ..."

Julien stands up, which brings the waiter running. He takes my jacket and hands me my purse:

"Now we're getting out of here. Don't forget that this is my town, and all the girls are waiting.... I'll have to hang around here a little before getting back to work, Anne...."

"Long enough to get drunk again.... I'm drunk, tonight I don't give a damn about going back, since we've been there...."

"Don't say stupid things and kiss me: hello, Anne ..."

Preoccupied with all our urgent conversation, we hadn't thought about that yet. An hour had passed, night can already be discerned through the oblique rays of sunlight; the people on the terrace have changed, behind new glasses in which bubbles rise, in which straws soak: yellow, orange, red, golden glasses.

"Your foot's not too tired?" Julien asks.

There is a whole past of gestures, of tender little rituals created by Julien around my limp: in crowds he goes ahead of me to make a sheltered pathway for my steps; he holds me under the arm, as though to lift me up, on the side where my walk falters, he shortens his strides to fit with mine....

But tonight, we're both convalescents: this term in jail is like a wound whose scar labels and unites us. Of course, we've both served painful time before; but never during it had we sighed, desired, with so much clarity and fervor: our dreams had been vast and slow. In order to create the moment we've just been through, we've spent three months, that "short sentence" that was our longest night.

The mother's house is at the end of a crossroad; it ends the town and begins the desert of the countryside, that land without frivolous growth where the heat stays buried in the beet and potato fields. To get there, we wander through the outskirts on roads full of grass and puddles; the cries of the ending day and the rays of the setting sun enveloping us in softness.

"I don't feel that much like going to your place, you know...."

This family's seen enough of me: the polite cordiality of Ginette, Eddie's exaggerated friendliness, make me want to scream. The mother is full of wisdom while also being candid; Julien can wade through the general constraint laughing, whereas I feel sort of like a whore. . . .

They probably think that I need Julien, are they afraid that he'll change keepers? Julien's family makes demands on him, tries to isolate him, would like to choose his women and his friends ... and this possessive anxiousness after absences he doesn't account for becomes a grumble when he gets back: Julien encumbers them, brings girls with him, and Ginette has to get up in the middle of the night to fix him something to eat. . . . Luckily, Julien doesn't give a damn:

"I'm my mother's son, right?"

"But I don't mean anything to them. I don't want to bother them, or have them bother me. I do like your mother and the kids, but ..."

"They've been talking about getting an apartment for a long time, but they sure don't ever seem to look for one! They like living with my mother, they can leave the kids with her and go out and have a ball. . . . And my mother ... she just loves kids. But I don't think she looks very well these days. I swear that all that's going to change: we'll start by taking her around, here and there, to get her out a little and so you can get to know her better. Later, we'll find her a little place where she can take it easy and where we can go and see her, just her. . . ."

I'm not sure that the mother would be happier that way, but I'm not about to ruin the serenity of the sunset with any dumb or uncalled-for suggestions. I have neither the right nor the desire to give my opinion, which anyway is only vague and unimportant. Julien can perfectly well take the mother, take me, wherever he wants: the main point is that I be able to walk beside him a little longer, beside or behind, but that I see him and touch him like today, as long as possible.

"You're going to come, I tell you. Perhaps we'll go and sleep somewhere else, but first I want them to see you, the way I see you tonight: Anne, my love, my only love …"

He stops walking, I stop too:

"Oh," Julien goes on, "I don't know where we're going, both of us, but we'll go a long way, for a long time…."

The houses are far away, the ground is under our feet like an island; invisible, victorious, birds are singing, it's the memory and oblivion of everything, it's St. John's Eve. Our kiss is as harmonious as nature.

15

The car has neither the mystery nor the disdain of a thorough-bred: so as not to attract attention, we chose a reliable old cow of a model, without panoramic windows, with sturdy parts; in it we feel neither intimidated nor exposed, it's like being inside a friend. Underneath me, the seat purrs along.

"Are you sleepy?" Julien asks.

"Oh Lord, almost dead!"

I'm stretched out on the backseat: the width of the car is exactly the same as my height. With my feet on the arm rest, my head on some rolled-up clothing, I feel comfortable, I float. The tops of telephone poles, trees, the dawning sky, the countryside melt into my eyes; I wait, without wanting to dive into it, on the shores of an ocean of sleep. I'd rather stay with Julien, look at his hair and the back of his neck, as during our first trip; we can sleep later, we have people to see first, friends who live at the end of the Pas-de-Calais and whom Julien wants me to meet.

Yesterday, we'd bought some tickets at a country fair and

won a lot of junk: a straw doll swings from the middle of the windshield, there are others on the front seat, along with a whole mess of road maps, clothes, provisions....

On St. John's Eve, the day before yesterday, we spent the night in the mother's bed, she'd gone upstairs to sleep with the kids; and ever since then.... To think that I used to resent sleep! As I'm perfectly willing to admit now, how much sleep matters to me! Ever since then, we've been on the road: the train to Paris yesterday morning; the morning spent trying out cars, in formalities, in red tape; the lunch with Julien's friends:

"Well, old man, where have you been?"

At the friends' house, the main dish arrives after the coffee, in the form of a liqueur come-on-and-have-another-little-taste, and interminable talk. To those laughs, to those jokes about the good old times, I have no recourse other than distracted listening, laughing along when I see everyone slapping their thighs, alternating between a glass and a cigarette until the stifled yawns and the headache.

During the evening, I'd made a hasty visit to Jean's to get some of my things: Julien had found me almost in my bare skin, I'd gone to him with nothing, but that "humble and total" gift hadn't excluded the necessity of changing my pants.

Jean had appeared to me to be something very old, very distant; since he had said good-bye to me on the platform of the station the day before, a world had been born; into the world where Jean continued to gravitate, I came back wearing a halo of sleepy happiness. I felt myself radiating in the grayness of that old room; the cries of the children in the courtyard, the music of the black neighbors, entered my ears without taking form: I couldn't find myself back there.

"Your eyes look happy," Jean said. "How you've changed,

since yesterday! And besides, it breaks me up to see you here so soon.... I thought you'd be gone for months...."

"I've come back to change my clothes, that's all. Help me, and be quick about it, I'm in a hurry!"

Joyously, I got undressed, I let myself be buttoned up the back, I let Jean sniff at my new skin: not because I wanted to do him a favor, but because "his happiness lay in knowing I was happy," I invited him with a cruel ill will to realize that I was just that, happy; and that he didn't, that he never could have anything to do with it. Jean, my storage space, my sucker, coat hook, good-luck charm if he wants ("And here's looking at you, kid, O.K.?"): that's the way I'd described him, in order to admit to him, to Julien; but Julien never pried into my life, what does it matter where I was or what I was doing yesterday, yesterday is dead and we are alive; tomorrow, the limbo of the future, after all.... How exhausting it is to think about anything! The trees are falling on me, the car is going down bottomless hills, I'm falling asleep....

"There's the ocean," Julien announces.

Immediately my desire to sleep goes away, and I sit up to look, as much as I can, at this unknown water, reaching to the horizon, the desolate truth of the deserted beach, the lagoons, the rusty rocks. I'd planned to go swimming as soon as we arrived, remembering the Mediterranean which was always so warm as soon as dawn broke; but under this gray and cloudy sky I feel more like putting on a jacket than a bathing suit.

We take off our shoes, park the car at the maximum, closest limits of the sand. Steps carved in the rock lead to the beach: I go down them painfully, my foot jangles every time it hits the stone, I cling to Julien. Our feet select the place for every footstep, until we get to the sand where, rescued, they can sink comfortably into a sticky and cold purée, sand, tar, seaweed, flotsam.... In our city clothes, dizzy with salt and wind, we walk along the tideline; I straggle, disconcerted by this indifferent setting that strikes and stunts me, this solemn and dead beach. Julien laughs:

"So, you don't feel like swimming anymore? Come, let's go back, I noticed an inn, up there. We need some coffee, after all this fresh air."

I fall into the car, I close my eyes, this time I'm not going to move again.... Julien comes out of the inn carrying a steaming cup: I drink, the bitterness of the coffee clears my head for a few more minutes, then blackness comes back in full force and flattens me for good. I however have the time to appreciate the soft heaviness of a rest which nothing, finally, will ever dislodge me from again, since Julien is handling it.

... The car is an island, in the middle of another beach, almost like this morning's, bordered by the same ocean, with the same gusts of sandy wind snapping against its body. In Julien's arms I cry, a little gust inside the big one, as salty, as desperate as the sea, I cry endlessly. Julien, completely surprised by what he's unlocked, tries to think up reverse, reeling words; but I can't, I don't want to be comforted. Right before this conversation, Julien had told me:

"You've got to listen to me, to hear me through till the end...."

And I'd answered that I was ready, that he could go ahead. I'd thought that I was sufficiently alert, sophisticated, tough; I knew what I was going to hear, but I didn't know that the reality of the words would be so painful, surprising as a knife stab, staggering, unforeseeable; as long as the women, or the woman, prowled around Julien like shadows without names or substance, the laughter of my faith and my youth had seemed reasonable, they passed across me without hurting me too much: put them down, Julien, you're absolutely right, put them all down.

But I don't have the armature of a confessor, I don't have the indifference of self-confidence. I don't have to understand or to forgive, I only have to channel off this hatred, this ferocity, which was born as Julien was talking, and which boil up and overflow now through my eyes, making me feel like screaming, writhing, torturing.

"But why do you care so much about all this, all of a sudden? You seemed to be so strong, so tough, you'd go off laughing, nothing seemed to touch you ... Anne, come on, since I'm telling you that that's all over, that only you matter.... Since tomorrow will be us!"

"But yesterday, Julien, yesterday.... When I think that she was there at the gate of the prison, where I wanted to be! That your first hours of freedom, your first love-making was for her ... no, no, it can't be true! And I was only always thinking of you, keeping everything for you, saving everything for the moment when I'd see you again!"

"But ... I thought you'd be there too, with Eddie. And he brought the other girl, more or less by accident, really. He didn't do what I told him to do, that's all ... please try to understand, Anne! She's bought off everyone at home, mother, the kids, she always comes with flowers, toys, clothes she has a good steady job, honest, she's my age, she's serious, upright.... So! They're trying to get me to marry her. The other morning, I was hoping that you would be there, truly, but since I had her on my bands, falling all over me ..."

"And where was I, during all this?"

"You ... you were my luxury, my secret.... Mother, who had her troubles during her youth, always tells me that if I stay with you, we'll always be pulling off something and end up in jail together.... She's a little unhappy that I keep leading such a bad life, she's my mother, what do you expect? ... And as for the other girl ... well, it was convenient to go and sleep at her place when I came to Paris, you know I can't very well go to a hotel. And at Pierre's and Annie's, you've got to realize that it wasn't always exactly fun.... And besides ... sometimes I was so tired...."

Into the huge shadows, a little star creeps: one day, perhaps. I'll be a rich lady and acceptable to the clan, I'll be able to lend Julien my bed, I'll take back my name.... Sure, years from now, when I'll have served my time and gone through my youth and when I won't have any other way of attracting a man!

Wait until you grow up! I've waited to get well and to be able to walk, that's already a long time, the star is too far away.... For the moment I'm here, my vision blurred with tears, but I'll adjust my vision, I'll learn how to see through the night. Maybe that other girl knows about patience like I do, maybe she's waiting for time to let her hooks sink in; of course, she has advantages over me of age and good character, she wouldn't be denied a marriage license.... But that's not what I want to destroy: I want to clean every crumb of her out of the present and the future, I want Julien to take back what he gave her with sweet gracefulness, as it's always like when he's giving, I want him to refuse her charms, never see her again.

"You can kill a body more easily than a memory," I say.

"But why kill her? I don't love her, I can't love her."

"Well, at least I'd make sure not to create any more!"

"What?

"Any more memories.... Look, if you tell her about me, or if she senses that you want to drop her, of course she'll find some other puppet, or some entirely new way of blackmailing someone. Don't believe in it, Julien, watch out for that kind of woman, I know them...."

I think of Cine, of the hideous cruelty that replaced the love and the tender tears, after our "divorce"; I think of Rolande, of Jean, and much earlier of the boyfriends of my adolescence; all those who lied to me and whom I pushed around with indifference in order to get further away, when it got down to it ... and I wonder if they hurt as I hurt today, listening with an infinite stupor to this strange wound beat; astonished, attentive, I discover the pain of love. A pain in my stomach or the pain in my leg I can put aside and move away from; but here there is no possible drug or dodge, the pain twists and shivers my whole body, it is myself. The details invade the image, up to the screaming point, up to the void. This time, in the impatient and assured me, that abstract and blue face of love, that pride, all that dies in the sand of the beach; I understand the terrible consistency of loving, and I am mad with pain....

Thank you, Julien, for having known how to hurt me so much. You put an end to unrealities, out of a body you made a woman's heart, those women whose beggar power I used to scorn, their mad attachments and servilities. Now it's I who's afraid of finding lipstick on your shirts....

"Let's go," I say, "they're waiting for us to eat."

As in a dream, another day passes, partly under the hot roof of the car, partly in the cool shade of houses, of tunnels; I'm too tired to count the hours, but all the same it seems to me that I could get through more days and nights like this; I am a reflex, a mechanism, time has stopped.

I give Julien the letters I wrote for him during those three months. While he's reading them, I wait, as one waits for a verdict, occupying myself by filtering sand through my fingers.

We've said good-bye to his friends, finally, after having numerous times drunk the last of the last drinks; and now we are lying down in the dunes, alone, without any special plans, on the verge of something, with that tenacious thread of joy which hasn't broken, hasn't let go since St. John's Eve, and has on the contrary been made stronger by the tears on the beach this morning, like a rope that shrinks in the rain.

"Your letters kill me," Julien says, giving them back to me. "Keep them for me. I still had a lot to learn about you.... Anne, forgive me ..."

"Forgive what?"

"That other girl: I don't see any other way of keeping you from crying more except by taking care of her right away. Come on, let's get going: we'll go back to Paris, I'll be at her place before midnight. You can wait for me in the car, and then we'll go to bed, for a day, two days, a week, as long as we want. I've been wanting to get rid of her for a hell of a long time, but it took this morning and your letters to make up my mind ... there's always that stupid desire to get away without hurting anyone, don't you know. But when you get right down to it, and it's shit or get off the pot, then it's just too bad: she'll have to pay for all the hurt I caused you."

"But it's three hundred kilometers from here to Paris.... Even though I haven't done any driving, I'm already beat; and you haven't let go of the steering wheel since yesterday!"

"You'll see, Anne, when we're together, at night.... Endless nights on the road, because it's absolutely necessary to get somewhere, or get away from somewhere.... Anyhow, I'm going to teach you to drive too, so you can relieve me or take the car back."

"Drive! How do you expect me to shift gears, with my stiff leg?"

"Oh no, you'll make it. And well, at those moments, you'll see how little it matters if you're tired and want to go to sleep."

I do not lie back down on the backseat: I sit in front, trying to watch the road, see it for what it must really be in actuality; but the trees dissolve into streaks of grayish night, while the intervals where the true night is get closer to the roadside and look like large dark tree trunks; indistinct shapes cross the road, leap and play, land on the hood and are swallowed up. The arch of branches drops giant dirty spider webs, which the headlights pierce and which re-form themselves immediately; right now, spiders are raining down on the car....

Julien must see them too. He fights off the night, starts up suddenly on the seat, falls back and grips the wheel, he hums, laughs and shouts, then he slows down slightly and snorts:

"Would you light me a cigarette?"

I light two cigarettes, aiming carefully, I slip one between his fingers. Mine burns me, gets away from me, I can't stop falling asleep and waking up again.

Finally, here are the gates of Paris.

I get out, shake myself off; under my feet, the sidewalk rocks and trembles like the floor of a car. I say:

"Let's get a room, come on: at this hour, they don't look through your papers very carefully anymore."

"Certainly not!" Julien protests. "I didn't drive all that way just to get a room."

"But you're going to pass out in her pad...."

"Don't worry about that! But you ought to go to sleep: I'll

finish this thing off and then I'll come back.... No, on second thought, I'd rather you waited in the car, in front of the hotel. The only papers I have say that I shouldn't be here, and ..."

"Oh come on. You can sign any old thing. Just for a few hours."

"... I'll be downstairs, at eight o'clock sharp. Have a good sleep, and don't forget to ask them to wake you up."

Without saying anything more, I let Julien get my overnight bag out of the trunk.

With leaden, icy steps, we head for the first neon sign that says hotel. My feet slide across the pavement, stick to métro grilles, my eyelids close; around us the witcheries of sleep put on a fantastic display, dizzying, dazzling.

... The bed, the table, the screen around the bathroom: I go from one step to the next, bent over, dragging, the room is as large as a desert. Once inside the bed, in my layer of lassitude, I shift around, I grope at the presence of the wall beside the bed; without actually sleeping, I have nightmares: people are running after me, calling out things that are flattering or deathly to me; I'm right ahead of them, but they don't see me. I stand in front of them, I shout my name, but I don't have a name and they all leave me without having recognized me, even those who claimed that they loved me. So, I run, I run endlessly through stretches of trees, of rocks and water: naked and black, I run away holding on to my youth, across hills bathed in air and light.

Where is the dream? Where will the tomorrows take me? This morning's depths, on the beach.... Bitter bubbles rise up out of them.... Come back, Julien. I'm waiting for you, in the serenity of this nice, soft bed.

"Come in! ..."

I remember that I'm naked, and I pull the sheet up around my shoulders. The door opens, the breakfast tray appears, carried by Rolande:

"It's seven o'clock, Madame."

She puts the tray on the edge of the table and disappears. Even she has not seen me. What are you doing here, skinny Rolande? You don't want to have breakfast with me? Even when we'd dreamed about it so often, swallowing down the lousy prison coffee together before each leaving for our workshops?

"Soon," we would whisper to each other, "it will be: two *filtres*...."

That girl who looks like Rolande is made out of yesterday's tears, day before yesterday's: no old tendernesses, no old bits of spite can bother me anymore, now. Rolande was the night light, the daylight is here, I turn it off. The sun, on the other side of the window, also turns off the neon lights and the fantasies, the windowpane is already warm; below, the street is coming to life.

Twenty to eight. I gulp down the rest of the coffee, along with the milk; before leaving the place I clean it up to please the maids, as usual. However, I'm sure I'll never come back here: tonight, another place awaits me, Julien is letting me into his mysteries, at last.

I'll get to know his territories, his stop-offs, his friends, I'll even get to know the Other Woman, why not? I'll make a little sister out of her, or else I'll introduce her to Jean. And me, I'll be on the road, always, as the shadow and the ornament; Julien's mark on me will erase all the old dirtiness, just as that second of flight, when I broke my leg, also broke off my last ties with shoddiness: my dears, good-bye!...

I open the window, I lean out of it.

One minute before eight: the roof of the car glides down the street, stops, just ten yards under me.... Julien! One minute to get down to you ...

I grab my bag, I open the door, I put the key outside; on the landing a man is standing, not very big, looking cheerful and gratified:

"Hello, Anne," he says to me. "I've been looking for you for a long time, did you know that? Come on, let's get going, I'll follow you. And don't try to run away, O.K.?"

I smile, Julien will see us go by, he'll understand that I'll be a little late and that it's not my fault.

Don't worry, just go: we'll find each other again on that luminous platform. One of us is again on a lower level; we'll have to climb and haul ourselves up step by step, peace retreats.... So what, at least I can walk: preceding the cop, I go down the stairs, hardly limping at all.